PETE,

DRINKER OF BLOOD

PETE,

DRINKER OF BLOOD

SCOTT S. PHILLIPS

PENULTIMATE DITCH EFFORTS
Bernalillo, NM

Cover by Beth Anthony-Stewart

THIRD PAPERBACK EDITION
December 2022

ISBN-13: 978-1542820776
ISBN-10: 1542820774

Penultimate Ditch Efforts
Bernalillo, New Mexico

This one's for my buddy Anthony Trifiletti, who kept my head out of the oven during some tough times.

THANKS TO:

Don Adams, Mary Bartsch, Rhonda Bloom, Adam Brown, Sam Carr, Lili Chin, Ceridwen Christensen, Scott Denning, Greg Freeland II, Gail Gerstner-Miller, Shannon Hale, Benson Hendrix, Nathan Hendrix, Axel Howerton, Liz Howerton, Brian Jay Jones, Sara Lehmann, Nathan Long, Victor Milán, John Jos. Miller, Richard Mueller, Rafael Navarro, Steve Riley, Patricia Rogers, Arelis Haskamp Romero, Joan Spicci Saberhagen, Melinda Snodgrass, Shannon Michele Thompson, Ian Tregillis, and Bob Vardeman.

Extra Special Thanks To Sarah Bartsch.

Author's Note:

Pete, Drinker of Blood was originally released as an eight-part serialized ebook. Some very minor tweaks have been made to the text for this collected edition.

1

The squirrel sniffed the thick night air, then scurried out into Durand Drive, oblivious to the threat bearing down on it. It was late — far too late for the squirrel to be out and about under normal circumstances, but this squirrel's nest was located near a streetlight and the beast had settled into an unusual work schedule. Two-thirty AM seemed, therefore, like a pretty good time to look for food. At least there weren't a lot of other squirrels to contend with at that hour.

At the bottom of the hill, the midnight-blue BMW Z4 turned onto Durand Drive, tires squealing faintly. Like many of the roads winding through the Hollywood Hills, Durand Drive appeared to have been laid out by someone dropping a rope from an airship and paving over the path it took upon hitting the ground. The driver of the BMW had no trouble hugging the twists and turns even at a somewhat excessive rate of travel, and the car speedily made its way up the hillside.

The man at the wheel of the BMW looked to be about

forty years old and seemed as in control of himself as he was the car. Not a muscle twitched without reason; his cold blue eyes never flicked away from the road ahead. Handsome enough to be a movie star, Carson Fitzgerald's smooth cool extended all the way up through his immaculate hair, which was swept up slightly on the sides, giving the impression he was sporting a pair of small horns.

In the passenger seat, pretty-pretty princess Darlette Aston stared at Fitzgerald, wondering why the impressive quantity of alcohol the two had consumed at the nightclub seemingly hadn't affected him. There was no doubt she was drunk off her shapely ass but Fitzgerald didn't even look buzzed. And he sure as hell wasn't driving like a man who'd been drinking all night. God damn, he was easy on the eyes, though — even if he *was* old enough to be her dad.

Darlette belched softly, then stared in wide-eyed distress at Fitzgerald for a moment, wondering if he'd heard. Born and raised in Los Angeles, the daughter of a North Hollywood strip-mall dentist, Darlette's only concern in life was to appear classier than she actually was, which, to be quite honest, wasn't working out very well. She played at being the rich-bitch spoiled party girl but her friends all made fun of her third-tier designer outfits and less-than-prestigious hair stylist. When Fitzgerald had approached her — well, okay, when *she* approached *him* but nobody needed to know that — at the nightclub, she figured the sexy beast could be her ticket to that long-awaited acceptance from her fancy friends. She vaguely remembered talking to him but she'd never managed to find out what he did for a living — it was almost like she was drunk before he started buying all those drinks for her. Intoxicated by his good looks, maybe. Anyway, a guy who looked that fine, dressed that sharp and drove a sweet ride like the BMW *had* to be involved in the movie industry. Producer, probably. And he was obviously on the prowl for a younger girlfriend.

Darlette smiled. Yeah, this guy was definitely her seat in First Class. She not-so-accidentally caught a finger in her too-short skirt, sliding it up a little further on her shimmering thighs. A little glitter to draw attention to those sexy gams had always served her well.

Glancing up, she caught sight of the squirrel in the middle of the road just ahead. "Oop — *squirrel!*" she shouted, a bit too loud, expelling a little spit in the process.

As Darlette stared in horror at the droplet of saliva she'd launched onto the BMW's dashboard, Fitzgerald snapped the wheel left, then right, deftly avoiding the squirrel but passing close enough to the creature to ruffle its fur. Darlette bounced off the passenger door, hitting her head on the window with an embarrassing *clunk*.

"Oop," she repeated. Turning in her seat to peer out the rear window, her dress rode up even further, exposing her panty-clad bottom. *Priceless*, the panties noted in silvery block lettering.

Outside, the squirrel wasted no time in getting the hell out of the road, disappearing into the bushes.

"He's okay," Darlette reported. "He's fat!" She grinned at Fitzgerald, sure he'd be impressed by her perfect teeth. Daddy might not be a rich Beverly Hills dentist but he kept her pearlies looking good.

Fitzgerald didn't look away from the road, but the slightest bit of a grin tugged at the corner of his mouth.

Wriggling a bit too obviously, Darlette turned and settled back into her seat, not bothering to pull her skirt down. "You drive like a... a super driver for being all

3

drunk," she said. "That was totally like, McQueen... McSteve or whatever."

Fitzgerald kept his eyes on the road. "I hold my liquor well, my dear."

Holy Christ, that sexy British accent, Darlette thought. His voice was warm and hung in the air like... *like the smell of chocolate cake baking*. All delicious and comforting. Only chocolate cake never made her want to have sex so badly. Well, not *always*.

Almost as if he'd plucked her thoughts out of the air, Fitzgerald finally looked away from the road and smiled at Darlette, causing her to giggle foolishly. She was in. *This*, she thought, *is the night my life changes*.

Maybe it was the liquor, but she didn't catch the menace in that smile.

Fitzgerald whipped the BMW through a hairpin turn, slinging Darlette against the passenger door once again. She yelped softly, but was quickly distracted by the sight of the Hollywood sign off to the east. Growing up in Los Angeles like she had, the iconic sign never meant much to her, but seeing it this close — and knowing Fitzgerald's house was nearby — counted for a lot. *A lot of cash*, Darlette thought. She'd have to put her ample skills to the test tonight if she was gonna hang onto *this* guy.

Darlette slid around in her seat as the BMW lurched off to the left, then came to a sudden stop, slinging her forward and bouncing her head off the dashboard with a comical *thunk*. "Ow," she whimpered, looking up at Fitzgerald. She giggled, putting her hand to her forehead. "I hit my face head. I mean" — she tapped at her forehead — "This thing."

Something went all squirmy in Darlette's belly as Fitzgerald leaned in close to examine her head. She sniffed at him loudly, like an animal rooting for food.

His examination complete, Fitzgerald looked into her eyes. "I find it impossible to believe any harm could've been done, my dear."

"You smell like... a *pie*," Darlette muttered softly, her gaze captured by those brittle blue eyes. "...That came from France."

Fitzgerald's expression — *Holy shit, he's not reconsidering this whole thing, is he?* — sent Darlette scrambling to cover her goofy pronouncement. "No — a really *good* pie! And it doesn't have to be from France."

Either satisfied with that or unwilling to listen to any further babbling, Fitzgerald wordlessly opened his door and extracted all six-feet-three-inches of himself from the BMW. *Never never call a guy a French pie*, Darlette scolded herself, watching Fitzgerald as he strode to her side of the car. The passenger door opened and Fitzgerald's hand appeared. Darlette, a bit worried that she was going to wind up walking home, took the hand, stumbling as he helped her from the car. *God, just let me stop embarrassing myself for five freakin' minutes.*

Fitzgerald's other hand settled on the small of her back as he steadied her. Something about his touch was like chewing aluminum foil, cold and tingly and not quite pleasant. As she looked up into his face, he gave her that smile again. Pressing slightly against her back, he guided her towards the house.

Somehow the old Spanish Colonial-style managed to *loom* even though, like many houses in the Hollywood Hills, it was set low on the hillside so that much of it was below the level of the road. As Fitzgerald led her through the manicured trees lining the walk, Darlette began to feel a little unsure about... *something*. The house? There was nothing outwardly creepy about the place — standard white paint with terra cotta tile roof, big as hell, luxurious. Exactly what Darlette was counting on, in fact. So why did she suddenly want to get the hell out of there?

Movement beneath one of the trees caught her attention and Darlette looked down to see a furry creature perched on its hind legs, looking up at the two as they approached. "Another squirrel!" Darlette pointed at the animal, wobbling as she did so. "It's like th' night of a thousan' squirrels an' shit." She scraped her tongue across her upper teeth, wondering why she was suddenly slurring her words so badly.

"That's a rat, my darling," Fitzgerald corrected.

"Eww," Darlette said, stamping her foot on the pavement in an attempt to chase the rodent away. It merely stared up at her, unperturbed, nose twitching.

"Now now," Fitzgerald scolded. "All creatures great and small."

"Not rats, though." Darlette kicked at the rat, missing by a mile and only avoiding falling on her ass thanks to Fitzgerald's firm grip on her arm.

As Fitzgerald pushed her towards the house, he looked back over his shoulder at the rat, gesturing with a nod. Tipping its head, the rat seemed to nod back at him before scurrying away into the darkness.

Darlette ambled along the walkway, grateful for Fitzgerald's gentlemanly guidance. She was pretty certain she'd never been so drunk in her life and was beginning to wonder how she was going to muster up the stability to perform the acts Fitzgerald no doubt expected of her. *Oh my God, what if I throw up on him?*

As they reached the heavy wooden double-doors, Fitzgerald gently leaned Darlette against the wall and let go of her, pausing for a moment, hands at the ready, to assure himself she wouldn't slide down to the tiled porch like a deflating love doll. Satisfied, he reached for the ornate doorknob.

Squinting an eye in suspicion, Darlette watched as he opened the front door. "Y'know, you don't seem like you're drunk at all." She pursed her lips, wondering why her voice seemed to be coming from the bottom of a deep hole somewhere.

Fitzgerald pushed the door wide and gestured for her to enter the house. She started to move but her legs had other ideas and she pitched forward, falling into Fitzgerald's arms. "I'm so sorry 'bout that," she whimpered into his chest.

Wordlessly, Fitzgerald half-carried her across the threshold. *Like in a storybook*, Darlette thought. The foyer was short and narrow, lit by a small table lamp sitting atop a Victorian desk. A few paintings that meant nothing to Darlette other than *fine art or something* hung on the walls. The antique chair at the desk looked *juuuust* right for Darlette's drunken bottom, however. She pointed towards it. "*Unnh*," she commanded, assuming Fitzgerald would translate. He eased her rump down onto the chair and went back to close the door.

Darlette fixed him with a pouty look. "I think you need more to drink."

The door shut with a low *ka-thunk*. "Don't worry, young lady," Fitzgerald said. He turned towards Darlette, smirking slightly. "I intend to drink quite a bit more."

Before Darlette screamed, she couldn't help but notice how clean and white Fitzgerald's fangs were.

2

The dance floor at Club Emoglobin was a strobing, candy-colored petri dish of undulating, pasty flesh — not all of it human. Thudding techno music boomed out at heartbeat-altering volume, vibrating the entire building and the bone structure of its occupants. Most of the pale patrons of the club were decked out in Goth finery, although the Steampunk look was beginning to infiltrate, bringing a little brown into the usual black and crimson. The bar was crowded with sullen would-be children of the night, unaware that the real thing gyrated within their midst. The drinks were served up by a tall, insect-thin pouter with ghost skin and stringy white hair that fell strategically across his heavily-lined eyes. In one corner, several overstuffed couches held a number of club-monkeys, male and female — although in some cases it was difficult to tell brother from sister — all heaped atop one another, wriggling and writhing like a sackful of corseted snakes.

At the door, IDs were checked by a muscular young woman who looked to be about twenty-five and appeared quite capable of folding a strong man up like a suitcase. Her Louise Brooks hairstyle framed a face that was nothing but sweet butter — lips like blood-candy, dark eyes flicking from driver's license to the pallid face of the latest Cure fan seeking entry into the club.

Outside, the throbbing music spilled onto the Sunset Strip, keeping the line of Emoglobin hopefuls edging forward whenever someone ahead of them got in.

Across the busy street was another world.

Suzi Quatro's cover of *Roxy Roller* filtered out from the doorway of The Starbucket as a liquored-up failed screenwriter staggered through the door, wandering off into the Hollywood night.

The Starbucket was a small dive bar, a holdover from the glory days of Hollywood when it was frequented by movie stars and powerful producers (the ancient wooden bar-top still bore a set of toothmarks where tough-guy actor Lawrence Tierney had once slammed a man's face down on it). The joint started a long, slow decline in the early 1960s, becoming a watering hole for hippies during the flower child days (The Starbucket's big claim to fame during that era involved an unnamable sex act performed in a front booth by a well-known rock god and two adoring female fans — fortunately, this left no marks) and eventually settling into its current state in the mid-70s, as a home for the downbeat, sad cats of Hollywood. The booths and barstools had all been re-upholstered in 2002 but nearly everything else was original-issue, and the jukebox — which played actual records, not CDs — hadn't been updated since 1979.

At first, it was that jukebox that kept Pete Tyler coming in. In recent weeks, though, it was the bartender who kept him planted on his favorite barstool of an evening. She'd started working at The Starbucket two months earlier, and in his usual fashion, Pete had tried to avoid getting too friendly with her. She wasn't having any of that, however, and as much as Pete felt he should stay the hell out of the place, he was flat-out intrigued by the young woman and couldn't help himself. Besides — there was the jukebox. Where else was he gonna listen to *Nude Disintegrating Parachutist Woman* by Budgie?

Pete's favorite barstool happened to be positioned perfectly in the one spot available past the edge of the mirror behind the bar. At the moment there were only a few other patrons in The Starbucket, but still, a guy had to be careful about these things. Pete looked to be about thirty, his slightly chubby, friendly mug topped by a short wad of curly brown hair. He was clad in jeans, button-down denim shirt and boots — his work clothes — and at the moment, he was staring down at an uneaten cheeseburger and a full glass of Coke.

"It ain't gonna eat itself, y'know." The bartender's Brooklyn accent snapped Pete out of it and he lifted his head, only to be stunned — as always — by how amazingly cute she was. "This makes fourteen times now," she said.

Pete stared dumbly at her for a moment, well aware that he was sporting an incredibly goofy grin but unable to control himself. The bartender was — well hell, she was foxy as all get-out, that's what she was. Maybe twenty-five, twenty-six, her tall, lean-yet-curvy frame was wrapped enticingly in a pair of tight burgundy hip-huggers and a Wolfmother t-shirt knotted up to reveal her smooth belly. Pete wasn't sure who or what Wolfmother might be but that was of no concern. The bartender's straight blonde hair fell around a face that made Pete want to cry himself to sleep, if he could just get past the damned insomnia.

"Uh…" Pete said.

"Fourteen times," the bartender repeated. "That you've come in here, ordered one'a the Starbucket's world famous cheeseburgers and a Coke, then just let 'em both sit."

"You've been counting?"

The bartender smiled. "A girl takes note of these things. Whatta you, on some kinda screwy diet and this is how you test yourself?"

Pete looked at the cheeseburger, the glistening grease oozing from it to collect in the bottom half of the bun. Desire welled up in him and his stomach grumbled softly. "Somethin' like that," he said. His watch — wrapped around his wrist by a broad, braided leather band — caught his attention. "Ahh boy, I'd better hit it." Rising from the barstool, he tugged his wallet from his back pocket. "And, uh, it's Pete. Uh, Tyler."

The bartender extended a hand. "Angie Burnett."

"Angie." Pete took the hand, shook it. "Like the Badfinger song."

"What's a Badfinger? You should eat, Pete. Wanna takeout box?"

Pete looked caught. "I… eat. But I've really gotta go. Lunch break's about over." He shuffled a couple steps back, not really wanting to leave at all.

"Lunch break?" Angie cocked an eyebrow at him. "Whatta you do all night, anyway?"

Pete hesitated. "You ever see *Close Encounters of the Third Kind?*"

Angie wiggled her fingers. "With the aliens?"

"Yeah."

"Not since I was six," she said.

Six. Good Lord. "Well," Pete said, "I pretty much do Richard Dreyfuss's job from that movie."

Angie shrugged. "I remember the aliens."

Roxy Roller faded out as Pete pulled a twenty from his wallet and dropped it on the bar, smiling at Angie. "No change."

Angie looked at the bill, then back at Pete. "That's a lot of money, Pete."

"What happened to the days when a man could stare

longingly at a burger and Coke and then overpay without being questioned like he was some kinda criminal?" He smiled.

The jukebox *cha-chunked* as it changed records. *Is it My Body* by Alice Cooper kicked in and Pete started for the door. Angie watched as he glanced back over his shoulder and shot her a little wave. "See ya," he said.

Smiling broadly, Angie returned the wave and Pete disappeared out the door. Sighing, Angie grabbed up the twenty along with Pete's dishes.

"Why don'cha just, I dunno — rub that guy's burger all over yourself or somethin'," sneered Suzanne, the scantily-clad, tattooed Suicide Girl wanna-be on waitress duty. She added a disdainful "Jeez," cocking her hip to put a period to the sentence.

"What?" Angie said, dumping the burger in the trash.

"God," Suzanne huffed. "You make it all obvious you like him. You practically" — she took a few seconds to dig through the vocabulary files — "*flang* yourself on him."

"I didn't 'flang' anything — "

"It's about playin' it cool, girl!" Suzanne emphasized the word *cool* by cocking her hip in the opposite direction. "Don't they teach you shit in New York?"

Angie poured Pete's untouched Coke down the bar sink. "Sure," she said. "They taught me that 'flang' ain't no kinda word."

3

Pete walked out of The Starbucket, frowning at the shitty techno music assaulting the street scene from across Sunset Boulevard. He tried to avert his gaze from Club Emoglobin and the frilly-shirted fruitbags milling around outside, but didn't have the strength. The female bouncer was standing near the Club's door, accompanied by a short, lean dude in a black mesh shirt, his dye-job raven hair moussed up into a ferocious pompadour, cigarette dangling from his black-smeared lips in affected cool. Pete could almost smell the clove above the car exhaust.

The bouncer and the short dude noticed Pete gawking at them. Sneering, they both shot him the finger. Pete returned the gesture and continued on his way, turning and walking down the next side street he came to, thankful to leave that techno beat in his wake.

Now that his interactions with the bartender at The Starbucket had gone past the point of introductions being traded, he really needed to get his shit together and stay the hell out of there. He'd been pushing things already by ordering food he couldn't eat every time he went in, and it had obviously drawn Angie's attention. Time to find a new hangout.

Damn, she was a stone fox, though, Pete thought as he approached his work truck. The white pickup was equipped with a service body bed, including tool boxes of various size running the length of each side. Perched atop the truck were two extension ladders strapped to metal racks. The Department of Water and Power logo adorned the doors.

Pete's stomach howled like an insecure cat as he opened the door and slid in behind the wheel. No putting it off any longer. He hadn't eaten for two days, and he was pretty sure the lack of food — using the term loosely — wasn't helping his inability to sleep. Starting the truck, he grabbed the mike on his radio and checked in with dispatch. They had him on one service call but he could easily blame any delay on traffic — sure, it was fairly late at night but it was also Los Angeles. Nobody would question it.

Putting the truck through a tight K-turn on the narrow street, Pete turned around and got back out on Sunset, heading east. Traffic was bumper to bumper on the Strip, as usual, and it took him a ridiculously long time to reach Highland Avenue. A left turn and a short distance later, he was on the 170 freeway going north, through the Hollywood Hills and the San Fernando valley beyond. The guilt over what he was doing was already tearing away at him, but he was just too friggin' hungry — besides that, if eating would help him sleep, then he'd just have to deal with the guilt.

God damn that jukebox, anyway. He'd walked past The Starbucket hundreds of times and never even gave the place a second thought until a few months ago, when he'd been on a service call nearby and decided to take a stroll down Sunset afterwards. The door of The Starbucket had been propped open that night — apparently there'd been a brawl and the mess was still being cleaned up — and Pete heard the cosmic strains of *Silver Machine* by Hawkwind wafting out above the smell of blood and beer.

Actually, now that he thought about it, maybe it was the smell that had inspired that walk.

At any rate, he had peered into the bar, listening happily as Lemmy's old band wailed the space rock. Stepping over the busted remnants of a table scattered just inside the door, Pete navigated the dangerous waters of the mirror behind the bar and took his now-familiar seat. Angie hadn't been there that night, but he *had* ordered one of The Starbucket's cheeseburgers and stared at it wistfully — so her count was wrong. It was fifteen times.

He came back to the bar a few nights after that, dropped two dollars' worth of quarters into the jukebox and punched in a bunch of selections, then turned to take his seat just as Angie came out of the back room. For about a week after that, he tried to tell himself he just dug the rockin' tunes but the truth was, Pete was smitten, and smitten was something he hadn't been in a good long while.

And now she'd introduced herself and he had responded with moronic babble. Suddenly, punching himself in the face seemed like a very fine idea. He hadn't survived the last — good Christ, almost forty years — by being stupid, and here he was getting all moon-eyed over a girl and putting himself on the spot.

Pete's stomach knotted up angrily, making him feel like he might pass out or throw up or both, not necessarily in that order. There were plenty of places he could've eaten in town, sure, and nobody ever paid any attention to a DWP truck prowling around, but he felt safer going out into the boonies where there was less chance of someone spotting him. Being seen eating was worse than getting caught with his schween in his hand, and fortunately he'd lived a very long time without ever suffering the humiliation of either.

After about thirty minutes on the highway, Pete exited in Santa Clarita and headed off into ranch country. Many of the properties in the area were regularly used as movie locations, but a lot of them still operated as ranches and kept a variety of livestock on their premises. One in particular had a good-sized herd of goats, and it was near this ranch that Pete wheeled the truck onto a dirt access road and pulled to a stop out of sight from the main road, hidden behind a stand of fruit trees.

Pete turned off the headlights and sat in the darkness of the cab, steeling himself for the task at hand. It never got any easier, that was for certain. He tried to imagine the way the others approached their, uh, dinner, but all he got were flashes of Angie in those hip-huggers. It was unfathomable to him. The others wanted to believe they were superior to 'normal' people, but Pete always thought that was a little too much like the Rush fans he knew.

An unsettling shriek from his stomach finally prompted Pete to clamber out of the truck. Shutting the door behind him, he tugged his pants up snug under his small pot belly. How the hell a guy in his condition could still be carrying around a bunch of chub was something he'd never been able to figure out. Walking to the back of the truck, he peered off into the night, worried that some ranch hand could be lurking nearby. Despite being reasonably sure no one was around to witness what he was about to do, Pete hunkered down stealthily and scurried over to the fence that surrounded this section of the ranch. Another quick glance around, then Pete climbed up on the wooden rails of the fence and hopped over into the field.

At this time of night, the goats were usually clustered up around the barn, which was positioned terrifyingly close to the main house. From his position near the fence, Pete could see the lights of the house were on, and the tell-tale bluish flicker of a TV set spilling from what he figured to be the living room window. He'd always assumed ranchers and farmers went to bed with the sun but this family of goat-herds sure as hell stayed up late — not once had he come out here and found the lights out and everyone asleep.

Spurred on by his grumbling belly, Pete — staying low in his half-assed commando-style walk — hustled across the field and up the sloping hill towards the barn. Something in the dark bleated anxiously, causing Pete to freeze in his tracks. It didn't sound like a goat. What if a big angry cow or something came trundling out of the night to attack him? Man, why couldn't this be as easy as pulling up to a drive-through window?

Cautiously, Pete continued on his way, constantly shifting his gaze from the house to the direction where that disturbing bleat had emanated from. A bare bulb in an ancient metal fixture was mounted on the front of the barn directly over the doors, and in its glow he could see a number of goats laying around in the grass, their legs folded under them. Pete looked toward the house, where he could now see the backs of two heads just inside the window, obviously caught up in the late movie. Taking a deep breath — although he didn't really need to breathe anymore, he'd kept up the habit — Pete turned back to where the goats were crowded together. If he went hustling into their midst it'd set the beasts off like a goddamn burglar alarm, sending up a cacophony of bleating and yelping. He picked out one particular goat, a large male, sitting off by itself about ten yards away from the others, just on the edge of the light from the barn. *Guess that makes you the take-out box*, Pete thought.

Just as Pete was closing in on the goat, something big shifted its weight in the darkness alongside the barn. Narrowly fighting down the urge to run like a striped-assed ape, Pete instead froze once more, hunkering down a little further. Whatever was back there in the dark began rubbing itself enthusiastically against the side of the barn, making a hell of a racket.

Pete looked back at the house. The two heads were still fixed on the TV. A loud snort spun his head back towards whatever was using the barn as a scratching post. He could see a massive black shape moving around, but couldn't make out any details. *Please, God, don't let it be a bull.*

Very slowly and very quietly, Pete lowered himself to the ground and crawled on his belly the last few feet to the goat he'd singled out. Thoroughly disgusted with himself by the time he reached his meal, Pete had to force himself to go through with it. The goat jerked its head back as Pete reached a hand towards it. "Shh," Pete said, gently petting the goat. Uncontrollably, Pete's fangs exposed themselves and his mouth ran with saliva.

"Sorry, little guy," Pete whispered. The goat made a pained grunt as Pete buried his fangs in its neck. It struggled slightly, but Pete continued to pet it soothingly and the goat calmed down, settling comfortably onto its side.

Pete kept a wary eye on that black shape pleasuring itself against the side of the barn while he fed. Always careful not to go too far, he drank only until he'd managed to ease the pain of hunger. Lifting his head, Pete released the goat and wiped his mouth in embarrassment. Wobbling slightly, the goat bleated in confusion.

"You'll feel better tomorrow, I swear." Pete patted the goat on the head one last time, then carefully made his way back down the hill to where his truck was parked, looking back over his shoulder the whole way to be certain the lurking snort-beast wasn't pursuing him.

What an awesome life I lead, he thought.

4

Even working the night shift, Pete always felt like he was racing the sun on his way home. All it would take was a lane-closing wreck on the freeway or running across a movie shoot blocking a surface street and he'd be in some serious trouble, and as a result he'd spent many an hour mapping out and test-driving various routes to his apartment over the years. His ability to get indoors before the sun peeked through the smog was the one thing he felt fairly confident about.

He hadn't counted on an eighty-year-old man, however.

Pete turned onto Dracena Drive at 5:23 AM and was delighted to find an open parking space at the curb only twenty yards or so down the block from his apartment building — he never had that kind of luck, and upon getting out of the truck, jogged back to double-check the sign to be sure they hadn't changed the street-cleaning schedule on him. Satisfied and amazed, he walked up the hill towards the complex, a 1940s-era three-story building that had once been a home for girls, presumably wayward. An ancient, yellowed, hand-lettered sign still hung in the basement laundry room listing the rules of the place, and "No gentlemen callers after 9 PM" held the top slot.

The godawful stink hit him before he even reached the walkway.

Garlic.

Pete stopped moving so suddenly he actually bobbed up on his toes for a moment, his eyes going wet and blurry, every nerve ending in his face jukin' and jivin' in misery. As he regained his balance and his heels hit the ground, he wiped his eyes and squinted at the bunches of fat, reeking bulbs strung in and out of the apartment building's door handles.

"*Nosferatu!*"

Mr. Stovall, sporting a sweater-vest over his pajamas — it *was* a chilly early morning in Los Feliz, after all — did the old-man equivalent of a startling leap from alongside the hedgerow near the walkway, losing his balance when his left slipper dislodged itself from his foot and went flying across the lawn.

"Hey, careful — " Pete made a grab for the codger's arm, but Mr. Stovall drew away violently, brandishing a small crucifix. "*Wampir!*"

Pete recoiled, shielding his eyes with one hand. "I just wanna go to bed, Mr. Stovall — "

"In your vile crypt!" the old man croaked.

"In my apartment," Pete said, gesturing towards the third floor while keeping the other hand between his eyes and Stovall's cross.

Stovall fiercely bared his dentures, thrusting the crucifix towards Pete, causing him to take a couple steps back. "Foul revenant!"

"Where do you get this stuff?" Pete asked. Resigned, he heaved a sigh, peered between his fingers at the old man — wincing a little at that cross — then assumed a Lugosi-esque pose, hissing rather unconvincingly. Spinning suddenly, he did his best Christopher Lee from the end of *Horror of Dracula*, sprinting across the lawn and yowling — softly, so as not to wake the neighbors.

Mr. Stovall watched as Pete disappeared around the corner of the apartment building. Lowering the crucifix, the old man smiled in vampire-fighting delight, then shuffled off to find his slipper.

Pete ducked around the back of the building, flattened against the wall, and poked his head out to make sure Stovall hadn't followed him. Then he looked up at his third-floor window, which seemed very far away.

I gotta move to the first floor, Pete thought as he began climbing the wall like a tubby spider.

5

As if being a vampire weren't enough of a cross to bear (so to speak), Pete had to be saddled with insomnia, as well. That was the one thing he'd really hoped would be different after he'd been turned — surely he could look forward to some pleasant slumber in a nice coffin, a pillow of his native earth beneath his snoozing head. He was disappointed to discover that sleeping during the day was even tougher for him than sleeping at night, and that coffin thing just wasn't gonna happen for him anyway — he'd tried it early on (in what Pete scornfully liked to think of as his vampire apprenticeship), but it reminded him too much of the time when he was eight and had wriggled his head and upper torso into a large carpet tube, becoming quite stuck. Those were, of course, skinnier days for Pete, but still, he was lodged in that tube for a good hour waiting for his friend

Mickey to fetch his dad. They'd had to squirt a bunch of Crisco up into the tube with a basting syringe until Pete was greasy enough to slide back out, and although sworn to silence, the first bell hadn't even rung at school the next day before Mickey spilled the beans and Pete became known as "The Crisco Kid" for the next several weeks. And don't ask about gym class.

Pete's studio (a.k.a. "no bedroom") apartment was well-guarded from the harmful rays of the sun — pull-down blinds duct-taped to the walls and blankets tacked up over the blinds just in case — but none of that helped with the undeniable knowledge that the goddamn sun was up, and even after all these years, he just couldn't get it out of his head and settle in. The springs on the twin bed shoved into one corner squeaked annoyingly as the Pete-shaped lump beneath the blankets readjusted itself in hopes of finding a comfortable position. Settling, the lump inflated slightly, then a sigh escaped from within.

Flinging back the blankets, Pete sat up, frowning. He scratched his head, ruffling his meager 'fro, and grabbed his watch from the bedside table, peering at it in the pale reddish light from the lava lamp bubbling away nearby. 11:23 AM.

Pete tossed the watch down on the bed and stood, rubbing the round wad of belly stuffed into his faded Evel Knievel t-shirt. His flannel jammie pants made a soft scuffing sound as he shuffled to the desk and switched on another lamp. The walls of the tiny apartment were covered with '70s-era posters — MOPAR muscle cars, Bruce Lee, and the one-sheet for *Jaws* among them. Hanging directly over the bed was a stunning black light poster of Mr. Spock.

Pete rested his rump on the edge of the desk, careful to

avoid damaging the mostly-complete model kit of a 1971 Plymouth Duster 340. One of the things disturbing his slumber was this situation with Mr. Stovall. The old coot was turning into a proper pain in the ass, that business with the garlic being the most aggravating example yet. Stovall and his wife had moved into the building back around 1986, so it was doubly irritating to Pete — he'd been there *first*, after all. That had to count for something, right?

Pete wasn't sure what had tipped the old man off to his vampiric capers — it wasn't like he'd been dragging victims back to the apartment, and certainly never after 9:00 PM (rules were rules). In fact, he couldn't even remember the first time Stovall had accused him of being a bloodsucking fiend. Six or seven months ago? And why all of a sudden, after living in the same building for over two decades? Pete wondered if the asswipes at Club Emoglobin got the same sort of treatment from their neighbors.

Shuffling over to the TV, Pete switched it on, finding a rerun of *The Match Game*. He flopped back in his comfy chair as Charles Nelson Reilly filled in the blank with a particularly bawdy double-entendre. Pete felt reasonably certain that no other vampire anywhere on the planet was engaged in that particular activity at that moment.

* * *

1:57 PM: The tip of Pete's tongue projected slightly from between his lips as he carefully razored the plastic windshield for the Plymouth Duster from the parts tree. The tiny windshield snapped free, dropping to the desktop and bouncing onto the floor. Pete, still in his pajamas, bent to retrieve it, groaning softly and for no real reason — he had somehow become one hell of a groaner in recent months, though, expelling air whenever he performed any sort of physical act that involved movement of some kind. He figured it had started as a subconscious effort to seem as human as he could, but now he couldn't shake the habit and it was starting to embarrass him.

As Pete sat up — deliberately holding back another groan — the newspaper clipping tacked to the wall above the desk caught his attention. Age-yellowed and dated October 3, 1973, the clipping sported the headline "Local Man Still Missing," above a photo of Pete, his sideburns even more impressive then and his 'fro significantly fluffier. The happily-smiling Pete in the photo leaned contentedly against an actual '71 Duster 340, but aside from the differences in facial hair and mop-top, his appearance hadn't changed a bit.

Pete gazed at the photo for a long moment. *I'll bet Angie would dig the car*, he thought, then forcefully shook it off and returned his attention to the smaller version of the Duster parked atop his desk. Picking up a tube of super glue, Pete ran a thin line of the fluid along the edges of the car's plastic windshield. As he moved to set it in place, the piece of plastic shifted in his grip, the glue smearing across the first two fingers of his right hand. Pete held the hand up, the windshield attached to his fingertips. He flicked his fingers and tugged gently at the plastic but it refused to budge.

Pete groaned once more.

* * *

4:19 PM: On the television, *Corvette Summer* quietly worked its magic spell. Pete, the plastic windshield still glued firmly to his fingers, dozed in his comfy chair. He snorted softly as a string of drool slowly ribboned from the sharp tip of his exposed fang to moisten the front of his t-shirt.

As the damp spot on Pete's shirt grew steadily larger, Mark Hamill climbed into a customized van with Annie Potts and the two set off to find Hamill's stolen car.

6

Wild howling split the twilight air on Hollywood Boulevard, carrying above even the car noise and rap music for a strange, terrifying moment. The pair of scantily-clad Boulevard girls weren't frightened in the least by the source of the wolf-like wail, however: a scrawny wino with two-thirds of a scruffy beard, sprawled on the sidewalk outside a store selling socks, knives and tiny replicas of the Oscar. The miserable souse was dressed in a far-too-short mini-skirt and tattered mesh football jersey cut off to reveal his wrinkled, leathery midriff. The mystery of that missing section of beard would likely never be solved.

"Get bent, creepo!" the girl in the beaded halter top barked.

The wino's howling abruptly ceased. "Put some pants on," he said, squinting one eye and pawing at his right arm-pit.

Both girls flipped him off and continued strutting down the street, their stiletto heels carrying them into yet another Hollywood night.

Elsewhere, Pete grabbed his keys, wished he could check his hair in the mirror, and started out the door. As he was locking up, his neighbor Trish walked past, carrying a sack of trash.

"What up, Pete?" Trish paused, holding the sack away from herself. "Y'got somethin' on your hand."

"Hey, uh, yeah," Pete replied, looking at the Duster's little windshield, still glued to his fingers.

Trish shifted her very attractive form in a very compelling manner to adjust for the weight of the bag in her outstretched hand. Pete tried not to think about it. "Did you know Mr. Stovall's telling everyone you're a vampire?" she asked.

Oh sweet Jesus, Pete thought. *That's all I need.* "Shyeahh, fssshh — I know, just 'cause a guy works nights, right?" He shuffled uncomfortably and gestured in what he thought might pass for a nonchalant way. *Ha ha, that wacky old fellow with his crazy vampire stories — well gotta go!*

Fortunately, Trish just smiled and went on her way. Pete tried to soothe his jangled nerves by watching her rump twitch as she disappeared down the stairs, but this had not been the way he wanted to start his night. Very consciously avoiding doing anything vampire-like, he walked out to his truck and drove to work, where he punched the clock in the most human manner he could.

7

Pete's first service call of the night took him into the Hollywood Hills to Mulholland Drive, where he somehow managed to become lost. No, scratch that — he knew *exactly* how he got lost; he had his goddamn head up his ass. First the whole Angie thing and now old man Stovall spreading the word to all his neighbors about the vampire up in apartment 322. How was a guy supposed to concentrate on his job when he had crap like that on his mind? He doubted he'd need to work very hard to convince everyone that Stovall was merely a kook — after all, it was a hell of a lot easier to believe an eighty-year-old man might be a bit nutso than it was to believe the chunky dude in the apartment down the hall liked to sink his fangs into tender flesh and suck out the tasty juices, but still and all, these things tend to fester in a guy.

A few minutes with a map and a quick call to dispatch got Pete back on course and he finally found the job site. Pulling the truck off on the side of the road, Pete switched on the flashers, got out of the truck and paused to enjoy the view from Mulholland for a moment. A lot had changed in Los Angeles since he'd been turned and he'd never seen any of it in the daylight. He didn't mind that so much, really; he figured a lot of that change wasn't nearly as pretty to look at as the lights of the city at night.

Pete reached for the bigger of the two extension ladders racked on the truck's work bed, then changed his mind and went back to the cab. He switched the radio on, tuned to the classic rock station, and spun the volume knob, filling the early evening with a little Humble Pie. As Steve Marriott insisted that he was, in fact, not in need of a doctor, Pete unhooked the ladder from the rack and set it up at the power pole. The tiny windshield glued to his fingertips made the task a little trickier than usual, but soon he was at the top of the ladder, peering into the transformer box.

Intent upon his work — more so than usual, determined as he was not to think about old man Stovall *or* Angie the foxy bartender — Pete didn't notice the winged shadow cast by the streetlights as it skimmed the top of his truck, faded across the road, then circled back towards him. He felt a bit of a breeze blow past — strangely, seeming to come from above.

It was the *voice* that finally caught his attention.

"Peter Tyler…"

Pete felt like his ballsack had been dunked in a bucket of ice water. Forgetting where he was, he took a step back, dropped —

Six inches. Then the well-manicured hand latched onto his wrist. Pete's momentum slammed him into the ladder, knocking it away from the power pole and onto the bed of his truck before it bounced and clattered onto the road itself.

"You're not pleased to see me, my boy?"

Pete stared up into the menacing smile of Carson Fitzgerald. The vampire clung head-down and spider-like to the side of the pole, effortlessly holding onto Pete.

"Holy shit," Pete said.

Fitzgerald's smile twisted.

A little *hunnh* sound escaped Pete's throat as Fitzgerald released his wrist. The vampire watched calmly as Pete crashed through the limbs of a tree and slammed to the ground at the base of the pole.

I don't need no doctor, Steve Marriott wailed into the night.

8

Pete tasted dirt.

Groaning (*again with the groaning!*), he pushed himself to his hands and knees, looking up to where Carson Fitzgerald slowly crawled down the power pole towards him.

"Still haven't figured out the whole turning-into-a-bat thing, I see," Fitzgerald chided.

Pete gingerly poked at his face, feeling the scrapes and cuts from the multitude of tree branches he'd made out with during his fall. The wounds were already healing as he got to his feet, staring wide-eyed at Fitzgerald.

Startled as the vampire leapt from the pole to land in front of him, Pete stumbled back, bumping into the side of his truck.

"Look at you, Peter — frittering away your eternal life as a common laborer." Fitzgerald *tsked* like a disappointed father. "And still feeding off livestock, I'd wager."

Pete was embarrassed to realize he was trembling slightly.

Fitzgerald glowered at him, fangs exposed. "Why do you continue to cling to your human morality?"

"I don't wanna be like you!" Pete yelped. Grabbing for the truck's passenger door, he swung it open and scrambled into the cab. Afraid to so much as glance at Fitzgerald, Pete slid across the seat, started the engine and threw it into gear, the tires slinging gravel and dirt as the truck peeled out and took off down Mulholland Drive.

Frowning, Fitzgerald brushed dust from his stylish slacks. His annoyed expression dissolved as the vampire went to mist, the tentacles of vapor suddenly whipping off down the road in pursuit of Pete's squealing tires.

In the truck, Pete glanced into the rear-view mirror, relieved to see Fitzgerald wasn't following him.

Oh wait.

Pete stuck his head out the window, looking back. *Son of a bitch.* The cloud of mist was hot on his heels, unhampered by the twists and turns in the road, simply flowing through trees or around other obstacles. Pete romped on the gas, skidding through another turn and very nearly losing control of the truck. He could probably survive pitching the thing over the hillside, but he didn't wanna risk landing his truck in someone's fancy living room.

Catching movement out of the corner of his eye, Pete was horrified to see a tendril of Fitzgerald-mist slithering its way into the open driver's side window. Frantically, he cranked the glass up, the vapor still slipping in around the edges. More mist crawled over the top of the cab, spreading across the windshield.

His vision obscured, Pete lost it. Hitting the brakes, he put the truck into a four-wheel slide across the narrow road, hurling it passenger-side first into a cluster of bushes, stopping just short of making that living-room dive.

The cab was filling with mist now, the tendrils worming towards Pete, going for his throat. Backed against the door, he fumbled for the handle. The door swung open, tumbling Pete out onto the pavement. *Woofing* upon impact, he found himself staring into Fitzgerald's snarling face as the mist went solid again, the vampire's hands clenched tightly around his neck.

A blur of movement, Fitzgerald whipped Pete to his feet and hammered him back against the side of the truck, rocking the vehicle up on two wheels for a moment and putting a dent shaped like Pete's ass into the work bed.

Fitzgerald hissed softly into Pete's frightened face. "Don't run from me, boy. It's a waste of everyone's time."

Pete's wiseguy-gene tried to fire but was overwhelmed by the pure, stark terror he felt, a fear so intense he wasn't sure his legs would hold him up if Fitzgerald were to let go of him. "I thought you were gone for good," he finally muttered.

"It seems after all these years I've developed an interesting condition…" Fitzgerald began. "Feeding on human blood barely keeps me alive now. Only the blood of another vampire can truly sustain me."

He still talks like a dick, Pete thought, a second before it occurred to him that Fitzgerald might be about to sink his fangs into his neck and start sucking.

"So I'm giving you an assignment," Fitzgerald continued. "Tell the others I'm back to reclaim my children."

"Wait — you want —" Pete was interrupted as Fitzgerald slammed him against the truck again.

"Tell them they can take their place as my servants — or perhaps my *cattle* is a better way to put it —" Fitzgerald grinned, fangs unnervingly close to Pete's throat "— Or they can die. Painfully."

"Can't you just make more vampires and leave us the hell alone?" Pete's question was met with a furious snarl, then chaotic movement as Fitzgerald transformed again, the flapping of his huge, leathery wings rocking the truck as he rose into the night sky and was gone.

Pete was quite correct about the state of his legs; he collapsed to his knees on the pavement, wincing at the rock that dug into his left kneecap. "Ouch," he quietly complained.

He stared at the little plastic windshield still glued to his fingertips and thought about his car for awhile before getting back in the truck and driving away.

9

Pete was almost to Club Emoglobin before he remembered his ladder was still laying in the middle of Mulholland Drive. It was going to be hard enough to explain the dent in the side of the truck to his boss — he didn't need to lose a pricey extension ladder on top of it. When he got back to the spot where Fitzgerald had first shown up, he couldn't find the damn ladder anywhere. After roaming up and down the street a few dozen yards in each direction, he finally discovered some kind soul had dragged the ladder to the side of the road, where it was almost hidden in the bushes. Pete looked over his shoulder the entire time he was loading it back on the truck, worried that Fitzgerald might come swooping out of the sky once again. With the ladder secured, he hopped behind the wheel and took off to deliver the good news to the other vampires. Truth to tell, he was more than happy to have delayed the task by going back for his ladder — there was very little he enjoyed less than dealing with those pasty-faced asswipes.

Finding a parking space on a side street, Pete locked up the truck and walked down to Sunset Boulevard. He almost veered over to the other side of the street and the Starbucket, but that way lay madness.

Especially with Carson Fitzgerald back in town.

It was still early; Club Emoglobin wouldn't open for a couple hours yet. Pete hoped this would spare him having to listen to any of that goddamn throbbing techno garbage they played in the joint all the time — bad enough to have to mingle with the vampires; listening to their music was beyond the pale.

And speaking of beyond the pale. Pete frowned upon sight of the club's buff bouncer chick leaning against the wall outside the door, puffing on a clove cigarette. Even back in the '70s when all his friends were passing the doobs at every opportunity, Pete had avoided partaking, not out of some moral misgivings at the notion of indulging in an illegal substance but because the smell made him feel like he was gonna throw up everything he ever ate. But the clove cigarettes the other vampires favored were even worse, the clinging, sweet odor like a cinderblock in his belly.

As Pete approached, the bouncer finally noticed him. "Hey, if it ain't the goatsucker," she said, sneering. She was decked out in a white wife-beater over black bra, a pair of black satin pants hugging her impressive legs. Well-worn Doc Martens rounded out the outfit, perfectly suited for planting up an unruly patron's ass.

"You're looking particularly masculine this evening, Pinball," Pete offered politely. Moving fast in hopes of avoiding chit-chat, he reached for the club's door.

Pinball stretched her beefy arm across the doorway, blocking his entry. "Not open yet."

"I'm not here to dance," Pete said, hoping like hell he wasn't gonna end up on the receiving end of a beating from the bouncer. He could practically see through the skin on her arm to the cabled muscles beneath. Getting beat up by a girl — even if she were a vampire — right out here on Sunset Boulevard, within view of The Starbucket's door should Angie poke her head out, would pretty much be the icing on the cake of one of the worst days of Pete's undead life.

Pinball took a drag on her cigarette, releasing the stinking smoke out of the corner of her mouth, tough guy-style. "What *are* you here for?"

"I'm playing messenger-boy for Carson Fitzgerald."

As terrified as he was of Fitzgerald and whatever plans the old vampire had in store, Pete still managed to take some pleasure in the way Pinball's pale features suddenly went even more ghostly. "Jesus," she whispered. Dropping her arm, she tugged the door open and led Pete inside.

The bar seemed quite vast indeed without the churning sea of club-monkeys packed inside. Elric Dreadsbane, the thin, mantis-like bartender, looked up from wiping down cocktail glasses and girlishly flipped his lank white hair back from his face, baring a single fang in a pouty smirk.

Ignoring it, Pete turned to Pinball. "Where's everyone else?"

She cocked her head towards the back, gestured for Pete to follow her.

As they passed the bar, Pete nodded to Elric. "Hey, Edgar Winter — you're gonna want to hear this, too."

Annoyed, Elric set down the glass he was wiping, dropped the rag on the bar, and followed.

Pinball led Pete across the empty dance floor. "You guys ever have, like, Bee Gees night in here?" he asked, looking around. "I could get behind that. Or *Dynasty* — you could do a little KISS disco party." Without looking back, Pinball shot him the finger and continued on to where an outstandingly extravagant set of dark purple embroidered drapes divided the main area of the club from the private rooms in back. Flipping the drapes aside with a magician's flair, Pinball continued on, Pete and Elric right behind her.

Set along either side of the black corridor walls were several blood-red doors. Pete could only imagine what kind of nonsense went on behind those doors on a typical night. "I didn't know you guys had nudie booths," Pete said. This time Pinball ignored him entirely.

Pete could hear muffled music emanating from the ornate wooden door at the far end of the corridor. As they approached, he realized what it was: *Bloodletting*, by Concrete Blonde. *Oh boy*, Pete thought. The door itself was etched with some pretty silly-looking runes; Pete figured it was supposed to be cool or imposing or some such, but he thought it looked like a rejected prop from a bad Italian sword-and-sandal movie.

Pinball stopped at the door, fixing Pete with a serious gaze.

"What?" he whispered.

"Don't be an asshole." She grabbed the iron door handle, turning it with a loud *choonk*.

Bloodletting increased in volume as Pinball pushed the door inwards, allowing Pete to enter. Elric was right behind him, followed by Pinball, who pulled the door shut behind her.

The sanctum sanctorum, Pete thought, *minus, y'know, the 'holy' part*. Not that he'd been inside all that many, but this was the most ridiculous vampire lair he'd ever set foot in.

Wall-to-wall retail-outlet gothic finery: flowing ornamental drapes adorning every wall, candles burning atop cheap metal holders, skulls and shit everywhere. Concrete Blonde blared from hidden speakers. It was like a high school drama class production of *Interview with the Vampire*.

Seated around the room on velvety love seats and JC Penney reproductions of Victorian-era antiques were three vampires, all of them staring in distaste at Pete. He knew two of them already: the chunky-but-foxy chick was Carmella Crimsonella, maybe twenty-five when she was turned, her fleshy (and quite ample) breasts packed tightly into a black and red corset that could've done with a bit of loosening to keep the boobs from exploding over the top like creamy lava. Her ruffled skirts — also black and red, of course — were gathered around her on the love seat she was sprawled atop, exposing her stiletto-heeled boots. The guy with the pompadour and the perpetually pouting lips was Bertrand Flagellamond — still wearing the mesh shirt he had on the night before, when he joined Pinball in flipping Pete off outside the club. His vampiric getup was completed by shiny leather pants and a pair of zippered boots that Pete thought looked very similar to those worn by the crew of the Enterprise on *Star Trek*. He was probably twenty-five, twenty-six, when he was bitten. The third vampire, perhaps even poutier than Bertrand (if that were even possible), looked familiar, but Pete couldn't quite place him. This cat was sporting a frilly white shirt with ruffled sleeves, unbuttoned down to his navel and tucked into his way-too-tight black pants. He looked like a nineteen-year-old session musician circa 1971, only vampired up.

"Really?" Pete said. "This is what you guys do, you sit around and listen to Concrete Blonde?"

The three vampires all made lemon faces, their black-lipsticked kissers pooching out even further than usual.

As the youngest vampire's pout receded to normal levels, Pete suddenly remembered where he knew him from. "Hey, I think I met you right after you got bit by one of these pasty losers — uh, Matt Stevens — from Reseda, right?"

Matt Stevens from Reseda sullenly pursed his lips once again. "I've left my human name behind," he said. "I'm now known as Francois le Sanguine."

"Fran —" Pete let out a little snort. Then he realized Matt Stevens was quite serious. "Wait, you picked that for *yourself*? You didn't lose a bet or something?"

Francois bared his fangs.

"What's that on your hand?" Bertrand asked, saucily flipping a twig of his pompadour in Pete's direction.

Pete looked at the little plastic windshield, still stuck tight to his fingertips. "It's a talisman. Supposed to ward off prissy douchebags but it doesn't work."

Carmella sighed, an act involving an unnecessary intake of oxygen that nonetheless had an impressive effect on her overflowing bosom. "Nobody here likes you," she said. "So I think the real question is, why are you bothering us?"

Pete flapped his fingers at the vampire babe, trying to force that talisman to work its magic. No dice. "Well, the *awesome* news is, I don't like you guys either. I'm here for one reason, and that's to tell you that Carson Fitzgerald is back in town."

The phrase *somebody crapped in their coffins* entered Pete's mind upon sight of the vampires' expressions. Bertrand squeaked out an effeminate hiss, causing Pete's eyebrows to climb. "Did that come outta you?"

Bertrand's lips wrinkled in a mega-pout.

"I don't believe it," Carmella said. "It's been, what, eight years?"

Trying not to stare at Carmella's chest but doing it anyway, Pete said "Closer to ten. I was hoping he'd stay in Europe but you know how much the music over there sucks. Uh, wait — maybe you don't."

"You talked to him?" She caught Pete staring and he snapped his eyes away towards Francois from Reseda as if the young fellow had suddenly caught fire.

"Not really," Pete said. "Mostly I listened and struggled to avoid shitting my pants."

"What's he want?"

Pete returned his gaze to Carmella again, this time dodging the eruption of boobage and looking directly into her heavily-lined pale blue eyes. "Us."

"For what?" Elric somehow managed to lisp while asking the question, despite the lack of s-words.

"Food, pretty much," Pete said.

The other vampires stared at him for a moment, rightfully puzzled.

"I don't think you said that in English," Pinball said. "He wants what now?"

"I dunno, it looks like somethin's gone haywire with the old man's plumbing," Pete explained. "He didn't go into detail — says suckin' down human blood is only an appetizer for him now, he needs to drink the blood of other vampires to survive."

Carmella and the others swapped a fearful look.

"Yeah," Pete continued. "So life as we know it is pretty much over. Fitzgerald wanted me to tell you we can either take our rightful place as an undead drive-through window for our bloodsucking master, or — you know — die screaming."

By this time, Bertrand was pouting so hard Pete thought his lips would fly off. "What are we going to do?" he whined.

"I don't know about you guys," Pete said, "But I'm gonna set fire to all my shit and flee the country." He looked at his watch. "In fact, I'm running late for that, so — see ya." He turned to leave, slipping past Pinball and reaching for the door.

"You know you can't hide from him," Carmella said.

Pete stopped and looked back at her, unable to keep his eyes from settling for an instant on that stunning balcony before moving upwards. "I look at it this way: right now, I've only gotta hide better than you guys."

He could feel the forceful pouts shooting his way as he slipped out the door and shut it behind him.

10

Feeling pretty good that he hadn't dorked out too badly in the presence of the other vampires, Pete stepped out of Club Emoglobin and started down the sidewalk, heading back to his truck. Then he stopped, looking across the street at The Starbucket.

Not a good idea. *Not.*

But he really could stand to hear a song or two on the jukebox to help clear his head. And who knew, maybe Angie wasn't even working tonight. Besides, if she were, it wouldn't hurt to tell her goodbye — not make a big deal out of it or anything, just tell her he's going on vacation, wouldn't be around for awhile. That was better than just disappearing, wasn't it?

Of course it wasn't. *But I'm too big an idiot to let that stop me.* Pete stepped out into the street, waited for an opening in traffic, and crossed.

Motorcycle Mama by Sailcat was on the jukebox and sure as hell, Angie was at the bar, pouring a drink for yet another depressed screenwriter. The waitress — the funky-looking chick with the tattoos — looked up from dropping off drinks at a table full of hep-cats long enough to make a sour face at Pete as he entered the joint. Not quite sure what that was about, he started for his usual seat at the bar.

Angie spotted him, shooting that terrific smile his way and canceling out the waitress's weird reaction — along with pretty much everything else Pete had on his mind. "Hey Pete!" She slapped the bar in front of his favorite stool, beckoning him over. Pete didn't see the waitress roll her eyes disdainfully.

"Hey, Angie," Pete muttered shyly, settling his butt on the stool.

Angie nodded towards the hunk of plastic glued to his fingers. "Whatcha got there, a little car windshield?"

Pete felt his cheeks go red. "Yeah," He tucked his fingers inside his fist as best he could, trying to hide the windshield. "From a '71 Duster."

"Superglue?"

"Yeah."

Angie grinned at him. "I think I can fix that for ya." She started towards the back room, waggling her finger for him to follow.

Pete got up, glancing at the waitress. She was watching

all this with an expression of disbelief. Pete gave her a friendly nod, causing her disbelief to evolve into something closer to abject horror. Satisfied, he took off after Angie.

Pete pushed past the metal door into the bar's back room, where Angie was standing at a cheap metal rack of shelves heaped with all manner of junk, digging through her purse. Boxes of liquor stacked ceiling-high lined three of the walls, the walk-in refrigerator and doorway to the kitchen occupying the fourth. Pete could hear the cook rattling around at his grill and realized he'd never seen the guy who cooked all those cheeseburgers he never ate. In the middle of the room was a ratty desk chair.

"Sit," Angie commanded.

Pete took a seat, the chair cocking itself at a weird angle as it took his weight, making him think the whole shebang would topple sideways. "Whoa," he said.

"That thing's busted, watch yourself." Angie found what she was looking for, extracting a small plastic bottle of nail polish remover from her purse. "This oughta do the trick."

Grabbing a filthy bar rag from one of the shelves, she walked over to Pete, seated cockeyed in the broken chair with one arm outstretched to counterbalance himself. He grinned goofily as she knelt in front of him.

"Whatta you grinnin' at?" she asked, eyeing him suspiciously.

"Nothin'. You."

Angie continued to eye him for a few seconds, unsure. "Gimme," she demanded.

For a brief instant, Pete had forgotten why he was back here with her. Then he awkwardly stuck out his windshield-adorned hand. Angie unscrewed the cap on the nail polish remover, gave Pete that suspicious look one more time, wadded the bar rag into her palm, then took his hand in hers.

Neither of them had noticed Suzanne holding the door open a few inches to peek in at whatever it was they were up to. The waitress almost looked disappointed to find them with their clothes still on.

Angie tipped Pete's fingers back and forth, finally settled on an angle of attack, and poured a little of the nail polish remover on the glue, the overflow collecting in the rag. "I could get in big trouble for bringin' you back here, I hope you know that," she said.

"Should I, uh —" Pete began, nervous.

"Hold still," Angie said. "You're a real squirmer, you know that?"

"Yes," Pete said.

Angie picked at the windshield, peeling it back some from the glue, then followed up with another soaking of nail polish remover. "Uh... this stuff is kinda eating the plastic," she noticed.

Pete just stared at her as she continued working the windshield loose. An electric, wriggly sensation was making its way throughout his chest and shoulders and he felt his ears go hot. "Wuhhh," he said as the broken chair suddenly pitched backwards, causing his right foot to jerk up and kick Angie in her left breast.

"Hey, ow!" She winced, grabbing at her boob.

"Oh my God," Pete said, reaching towards the injured area. Angie's eyes widened as the hand came at her. Realizing what he was doing, Pete quickly yanked his hand back. "Sorry — I'm sorry. Oh my God, am I sorry."

Playing it up, Angie grimaced as she gently rubbed her offended breast. "Man," she said in a pained voice, pleased to see Pete's eyes zip away in embarrassment.

In the doorway, Suzanne quietly smacked her palm against her forehead.

"I'm really sorry," Pete said again.

"Dude, you owe me for that." The corner of Angie's mouth cocked upwards in a wry smile as she went back to work on the windshield.

"Okay." Pete figured he couldn't really argue. "Uh, what do I owe you?"

"Taa-dahhhh!" Angie crowed, holding up the tiny windshield, finally freed from Pete's fingertips. Pete held the fingers in front of his face, wiggling them.

"Now you owe me double," Angie said. "I'm thinkin' maybe dinner."

Uh-oh. Pete visibly stiffened in the chair, nearly losing his balance once again.

Off the look on Pete's face, Angie hurriedly added "I'll eat cheap, though, so don't sweat it."

This is exactly why he shouldn't have set foot in The Starbucket. He should've just gone home, packed his things, and gotten the hell out of town while the getting was good. Even if it meant wearing that damn windshield on his fingers for the rest of his life, or until he figured out that something as simple as nail polish remover would do the trick, whichever came first.

"Dinner? Like, *right now?*" He asked, struggling to keep from fidgeting and falling out of that chair.

Angie smiled, enjoying his boyishly-silly reaction. "No, dude — I'm at work. But I'm off tomorrow night."

Just say no. That's all you've gotta do, one simple word: No.

"Okay," Pete said.

"Cool," Angie said.

In the doorway, Suzanne — thoroughly disgusted by now — let the door swing shut as she returned to her work.

Her task completed, Angie rose, standing in front of Pete and smiling down at him. Looking up at her friendly expression, Pete completely understood why he hadn't gone home and packed. "Hey, y'know what," he said, feeling slightly giddy. "Speaking of dinner, could I get one of those burgers? I think it's time I finally ate one instead of just staring at it."

"I can do that," Angie said. "Waitaminnit, though — I'm not gonna be enabling you to go off some kinda special diet or somethin', am I?"

If you only knew, Pete thought. "Kind of, but I take full responsibility."

"All right." Angie cocked a thumb towards the door. "Back out front witchoo. I'll have it there in a minute."

Leaving Pete to gingerly extract himself from the dangerous chair, Angie poked her head into the kitchen and ordered up his cheeseburger. He caught a glimpse of the cook, mostly hairnet, grease-stained apron and forearms like Popeye.

As Pete pushed the door open and re-entered the bar's main room, that waitress was glaring at him like he'd slept with her mom and didn't cuddle afterwards. Maybe she'd figured out what he was? Or was he just being especially paranoid thanks to old man Stovall? All Pete knew for sure is that he didn't want thoughts of that sort crunching his delightful Angie-induced buzz. Going to the bar, he plopped down at his regular spot, wishing he could lean over, look in the mirror, and see the big goofy grin he was sporting. Resting his elbows on the bar, he rubbed his windshield-free fingers with his thumb and enjoyed the loud-as-hell monster

Speed King from the first Ian Gillan-era Deep Purple record.

Moments after the song was over, Angie banged through the door to the back room, carrying that big, sloppy cheeseburger. She presented the plate to Pete like she was showing off a car on *The Price Is Right*, set it down, then drew him a tall Coke.

Pete gazed wistfully at the cheeseburger, entirely lost in the moment. "Just like normal people," he said softly.

"What?" Angie asked, setting the glass of Coke in front of him.

Oops. "Huh?" Pete said.

Ignoring Angie's look of confusion, he picked up the burger, eyeballed it for a long moment, then sank his teeth into the soft bun, through the gooey cheese, and into that slab of greasy, delicious beef.

11

Bent over in the alley behind The Starbucket, Pete made dinosaur sounds as he violently horked up the entire contents of his body.

For some reason, the act of vomiting had caused his fangs to protrude, only adding to his embarrassment. Hands on knees, he watched as a rivulet of slobber shimmied its way down from his left fang. Straightening, he wiped his face with the back of his hand, then spent the next few seconds trying to sling the ribbon of drool loose from his hand before finally wiping it on his pants. He looked furtively up and down the alley, then started walking. After a dozen steps, a spasm hit him, folding his body in half again as he threw up once more, yowling thunderously.

He remained in that position for quite some time, elbows on knees and breathing hard. After getting his shit together enough to retract his fangs, he toddled off on his way. As he rounded the corner and started along Sunset Boulevard, the agony in his belly struck again, doubling him over with — well, not the dry heaves, exactly, but the only-somewhat-moist heaves, certainly.

Jesus, Pete thought, leaning against the wall and deliberately avoiding eye contact with the appalled pass-ersby. *I only ate one bite of the goddamn burger — how the hell can I still be puking?*

The walk back to his truck continued in a similar fashion — stumble along for a few steps, croak and puke, recover, walk a bit further. At least he felt like he fit in pretty well with some of the Sunset Strip regulars.

Finally, after what seemed like an hour, Pete arrived back at his truck. He leaned against the vehicle for a few moments, staring at the dent in the side where Fitzgerald had slammed him into it. When he felt reasonably confident that he was done vomiting, he got in the truck and drove off, heading east up Sunset for a bit, then snaking his way up to Hollywood Boulevard, where he continued eastward.

What in the hell had he been thinking? The whole idea was to go into The Starbucket, tell Angie he was leaving town for awhile, then get out of there and never look back — not set up a freaking dinner date. And how was *that* gonna work, anyway? *Oh, hey, no — you go ahead and tuck in, I'll just watch, because I'm actually a vampire and if I eat people food I'll throw up all over you for the next forty minutes.*

"I'm an idiot," Pete muttered.

Looking out the driver's side window, he spotted Griffith Observatory flashing past between buildings. It'd been one hell of a long time since he'd been to the Observatory — just one more thing he'd given up or lost unwillingly thanks to the vampire horseshit. Man, he'd always loved hanging out up there, too.

Gazing up at the place, his thoughts drifted back to that October night in 1973, when he could still eat a cheeseburger in the daylight. The sun was on its way down and somebody was cranking *Co-Co* by Sweet on their car stereo, almost certainly via 8-Track tape, as Pete rolled the Sassy Grass Green 1971 Plymouth Duster 340 into the Observatory parking lot. Cruising slowly through the steel beauty pageant of classic (well, *soon to be:* tonight they were — for the most part — new) cars and the assortment of hippies, gearheads, and surfers gathered to enjoy the show, Pete finally felt like part of the human race. He'd been hanging out at impromptu car shows like this for years, of course, but his innate shyness — not to mention lack of an automobile of his own — had always kept him on the fringes. Pete wasn't the sort to define himself by the car he drove, but sitting behind the wheel of the Duster, he couldn't help but feel a bit like a rock star. Sure, she was a couple years old, but she was new to Pete, and judging from the approving smiles from the foxy ladies strolling by, he wasn't the only one who thought the car kicked all kinds of ass.

He found a parking space and backed the Duster in. The muscular engine throbbed, growled, then faded to silence as Pete shut it down, grinning like hell at the sleek dashboard and sliding his thumbs along the curve of the steering wheel.

"Right on, brah!" Pete's buddy Hector, twenty-two and the spitting image of a young Tommy Chong, strode towards the Duster, swigging from a can of PBR in his left hand and carrying another in his right. As Pete opened the door and got out, Hector tossed him the extra can of beer. "I can't believe it, you finally got her!"

The beer made a frothy *fweesh* as Pete popped the top, tossing the ring into a trash can nearby. "Just picked her up," he said, watching Hector run his fingers delicately along the car's curves, caressing the Detroit steel like it fell out of this month's *Playboy*. "Two years of saving, but she's mine now."

Hector put his face close to the metal, gazing along the lines of the front fender. "She's hot as love, man." Grinning, he spun to face Pete. "So who's gonna be the lucky chick gets the first ride?"

Leaning against the car, Pete chuckled softly, his cheeks reddening. "Pff, I dunno, I'm... I'm just glad to have her."

Hector tugged an Instamatic camera from one of the many pockets adorning his painter's jeans. "We gotta document this moment, man." Eyeballing Pete through the viewfinder, Hector lined up the shot. "Say *weeeeed*."

Pete awkwardly grinned as Hector snapped the photo, a picture that would become famous in the papers in coming days.

As he blinked away the effects of the flashcube, Pete was sure he was seeing an angel straight out of Heaven drifting towards him in the lingering glare. His vision clearing, he was stunned to find the angel was in fact a hippie chick, perhaps the hottest he'd ever laid eyes on: glossy black hair ironed to whip-straight perfection, flowing over her shoulders and the flower-print blouse knotted seductively beneath her spectacular breasts. Her smooth belly dipped into low-slung hip-huggers that flared out wide at the bottoms of the legs, hiding her feet and making it seem as if she were gliding across the pavement…

Towards Pete.

Wait, that can't be right. In fact, so certain was he that she couldn't possibly be headed for him, he took a moment to look around for the lucky guy. Hector? Maybe. Pete looked at the angel again. She gave him a smile.

"My man, I do believe you're about to put the stress test on the back seat of this fine automobile," Hector whispered.

The hippie-angel-sweet-foxy-mama walked right up to Pete, standing mere inches away from him, still smiling that smile. "Hi," she said. "I'm PJ." She leaned in even closer. "Sweet ride," she observed, not looking at the car.

"It — it's a car," Pete pointed out. "My car. It, uh…" He punctuated this scintillating bit of conversation with a shrug.

"Take me for a ride," PJ said, using a very interesting assortment of words.

It was difficult for Pete to focus on his driving what with PJ draped all over him, nuzzling his groovy sideburns and sliding her hands into areas that hands — other than his own — had not often traveled upon Pete's person. Occasionally she'd stop groping him long enough to give directions, waving him through various turns until they were finally on Bronson, headed deeper into the Hollywood Hills.

Eventually she directed him to park on the side of the road, where she reached across him to open the driver's side door, then slowly slid over his lap (finding the path a bit, *ahem*, bumpier than she might have expected) and got out of the car. Leaning in the open door, she playfully began untying the knot in her blouse, directly in front of Pete's stunned face.

"C'mon," she whispered, flicking her blouse open ever-so-slightly to give Pete a glimpse of the ghostly-pale flesh beneath. Giggling, she scampered away past the front of the Duster.

Awash in the realization that his good fortune was, in fact, a very real thing indeed, Pete sat watching in wonderment as PJ sauntered off, heading up a dirt trail that curved away around a hillside. A flirtatious glance back over her shoulder just before she disappeared around the bend finally got him moving and he nearly fell out of the car in his haste to catch up. Stumbling up the trail in the dark, Pete tripped over something and dropped to his hands and knees, scuffing the skin on his palms. Looking up as another giggle burst from PJ, he marveled at the way she scurried along the trail, sure-footed as a particularly tantalizing mountain goat.

"Wait," Pete said, getting to his feet. "Wait up!"

PJ's giggling lured him on, faster this time. He trotted along a dozen yards or so behind the girl, unable to catch up, her pale skin like a beacon. He could see her blouse fluttering open as she led him further up the hill, then down again.

Hitting the bottom of the trail, she took off across the flat ground, shouting back over her shoulder. "C'mon, hurry!"

Pete nearly fell again, slid a few feet in the dirt, caught his balance and increased his speed. He was a little concerned that he was gonna be too wiped out from all the running to perform his manly duty once he caught up with the girl, but crossed his fingers and hoped for a second wind. As he reached the bottom of the trail, he realized PJ was heading for the instantly-recognizable blackness of Bronson Cave. "Holee..." he said out loud.

Up ahead, PJ paused, smiling back at him as she fiddled with the loose ends of her blouse.

"Are you tellin' me we're gonna get it on in the *Batcave?*"

Pete gleefully asked, almost overwhelmed by the notion.

Smirking haughtily, PJ answered the question by peeling off her blouse and tossing it over her shoulder as she ran into the cave, disappearing in the darkness.

Pete suddenly felt an inexplicable urge to hoof it back to his car as fast he possibly could, get in, and drive like hell out of there. But there was an unbelievably foxy half-naked (possibly more than half, by this point) hippie chick in that cave, waiting for him to get in there and take care of whatever business needed taking care of. And let's face it, Pete's business had been pretty bad for some time now. Buying the Duster had expanded his customer base by the significant factor of one, and it would be beyond foolish to blow the deal at this stage. Chalking up his trepidation to having seen Bronson Cave in about nine-thousand old monster movies, Pete wrangled the small amount of courage he possessed into a tight little ball and more or less scampered the rest of the way to the cave entrance. Pausing for a moment to peer excitedly down at PJ's blouse resting on the ground and savor the anticipation of what was about to take place, he entered the Batcave.

Not an authentic cave at all, but a tunnel cut through the hill back in the days when Bronson Canyon was a rock quarry called Brush Canyon, the Batcave was impossibly dark. Fumbling around with hands out in front of him, Pete should've been able to see some kind of light from the other end of the tunnel. This was just plain weird. "PJ?" he whispered, the hollow sound of his voice inside the cave freaking him out even more.

His right hand came up against something soft and he jumped back, nearly letting out a shriek. Then it occurred to him what he may have felt, and he groped blindly around, hoping for another go at it. After a few seconds, his hand was full of warm, supple flesh once again. *Lessee*, Pete thought, shifting the hand to the right. Nope. Back over to the left, past that delectable mound... *There it is.* "Um, hi," he said to PJ's right breast, cupped gently in his hand. His eyes finally adjusting somewhat to the darkness, he took in the view, smiling.

PJ let out a throaty growl, shoving Pete back into the rock wall and sharply banging his head. Before he could react, she clamped her wide-open mouth over his, turning his pained *Ow* into more of a satisfied *Erf*. This was followed by an *Umf* and two or three *Mmmf*s. They made out rather furiously for several moments, long enough for Pete to feel like he was beginning to get his chops back.

Until something sharp jabbed his frolicking tongue.

This time the *Ow* made it out quite clearly as Pete pulled away from the girl. Sticking his tongue out stupidly, he felt the tip of it with his fingers.

"What? *C'monnn*," PJ implored, tugging at him, trying to get the action going again.

"Um..." Pete mumbled around his injured tongue. "This sounds dumb, but — you got somethin' sharp in your mouth."

Even in the darkness he could see the dubious look she was giving him. *I do believe I just blew it*, he thought, remembering to put his tongue back in his mouth.

PJ smiled.

Pete stared, fully aware of the blank expression he had to be sporting. *Well*, he observed. *That would explain it.* He hadn't noticed it during any of the countless other smiles she'd shot his way, but the chick had some seriously pointy teeth.

Deciding that a bit of caution was all he needed in order to safely navigate those ferocious chompers, Pete was on his way back in for more smooching when an odd *crack* split the silence of the cave, followed by sudden, blinding light, like Hell's own road flare. Pete instinctively threw an arm up to shield his eyes, while PJ recoiled like she'd been kicked, moving to Pete's side and practically cowering behind him.

"Jesus, what the hell!" Pete squinted into the light. Instead of the cop he'd expected to see, he could make out a tall, thin dude, flamboyant psychedelic embroidery crawling up the legs and sleeves of his matching white bell-bottoms and jacket, shirtless torso befurred with precisely the right amount of hair and not one curl more, his shoulder-length locks somehow shaggy and impeccable all at once, the flare — or whatever it was — he held throwing bizarre, flickering shadows of his narrow form across the cave walls.

"*What is this?*" Carson Fitzgerald demanded.

PJ made herself very tiny behind Pete. Feeling protective despite his fear, Pete tried to puff himself up some, a threatening cave-toad. "What's the deal, man?"

The mysterious rocker ignored the question, scowling past Pete to where PJ struggled to hide. "I brought him for you, Master!" she said.

Whoa, hang on a second — *Master?* What kind of screwed-up shit was going on here? *Dammit*, Pete thought. *Just my luck to go and get myself wound up with a couple of Hollywood Hills sex freaks.* If he didn't get out of there but fast, he'd be lucky if the evening didn't end with him getting spanked with reel three of *The African Queen* or something. Why couldn't anything ever be easy?

"All right, folks," Pete began, sidestepping around PJ and gearing up to make his exit. "I think it's safe to say you

guys are barkin' up the wrong tree, 'cause I'm not into —"
Pete's polite attempt to bow out trailed off as the rocker
dude pulled a wicked knife, the ornate silver blade practically glowing under the brilliant light from the flare.

Pete had all of about three seconds to wonder exactly
where the hell the guy had been carrying the knife in those
tight pants before he suddenly darted forward, making a
lightning-quick slash with the blade.

PJ didn't even have time to scream. Pete watched in
horror as blood fountained from her throat, her eyes staring
widely at his. A grotesque gurgle escaped the girl's lips and
her head toppled sideways, dropping to the ground with a
sickly thud.

"I have little tolerance for infidelity," Fitzgerald calmly
stated.

Running seemed like a very good idea, but the thought
had barely reached Pete's legs before the vampire was on
him. The pain was indefinable, overwhelming, searing as the
fangs punctured his throat, but even as he felt the blood
being leeched from his body, a soothing numbness settled
over him.

Strangely, it occurred to Pete that he'd owned the Duster
for all of about two hours before a guy wearing Jimmy
Page's clothes started sucking his blood.

* * *

Pete was wrong; he had one more bout of heaving left in
him. Swerving the truck over to the side of the road, he
threw the door open and let fly, roaring into the Hollywood
night. Not a damn thing in there to come up, but for a little
spit. Staring at the tiny wet spot on the pavement below, he

realized he was still on the damn clock, and Water and Power would wait for no man. Or vampire.

Pete sat up and scrounged the glove box for a napkin to wipe his face, then picked up the mike to check in with dispatch. Across the street, a four-foot-tall wino wearing plastic Incredible Hulk fists and bib overalls was shrieking something unintelligible at him. Pete gave the fellow a friendly wave, causing the little souse to flee in apparent terror, his stubby legs carrying him away down the Walk of Fame.

Truly, Pete thought, keying the mike, *I am — and always have been — an idiot.*

12

Ike, the rotund night security man on duty in the empty lobby of the Department of Water and Power, picked gently through the strands of his graying beard in search of the lost chunk of chocolate he was certain he could smell lurking there. He'd topped off his delicious dinner of a 4x4 and animal fries from In-N-Out Burger with a package of Ding Dongs, and a bit of the glossy, wax-like coating must have escaped into his chin-scruff. Now, hours later, the occasional whiff of misplaced chocolate was distracting him from his duties — or more specifically, the sides he was trying to memorize for the audition he had lined up the next day. He'd be reading for the role of 'Beefy Bus Driver' in a low-budget horror movie, and his hopes were high that the role would propel him to further glory in similar productions.

Feeling a foreign object amidst his fur, Ike carefully zeroed in on it and tweezed it between the tips of his thumb and forefinger. Extracting the bit of detritus, he squinted at it carefully to be sure it was chocolate and not a bug. Satisfied that it was indeed edible, Ike flicked out his tongue to snag it. As the chunk of waxy goodness melted on the tip of his tongue, the buzzer at the front door sounded, signaling someone entering their security code. Another buzzer sounded as the magnetic lock released, and Pete Tyler entered, the door swinging shut behind him.

"How goes it, Pete?" Ike asked, lifting his hand in a half-hearted wave. "You okay? You look a little shook up."

"Yeah, I'm — I've got a… thing," Pete said, approaching the security guard's desk. "Harry around?"

"When is he not? You know where to find him."

Pete nodded at the sides on Ike's desk. "Got another audition?"

"Tomorrow, yeah. Feelin' good about it, though."

"Good luck, man," Pete said as he started off towards the door that led to the inner workings of DWP.

"Don't let stuff get you down, Pete — the sun's always gonna rise again," Ike offered helpfully.

Smiling weakly, Pete shot him a nod and went on his way. He hoped Ike would get whatever part it was he'd be reading for — the security guard had been trying to break into acting for years and had never had any luck with it. Pete wondered if ambition wasn't more of a curse than vampirism — he could barely remember back to the days when he dreamed of doing something with his life, but he could still taste the disappointment he'd felt when things didn't go the way he'd hoped. Maybe getting bitten by Fitzgerald saved him from a life of that.

Jeezus, Pete thought. *I sound like the mopey assholes at Club Emoglobin.* The last thing he needed was to wind up stewing in his own misery like the other vampires — that was surely a one-way ticket to sitting around listening to Bauhaus or The Smiths or some damn thing.

Hooking a left, Pete walked to the end of the corridor, where he pushed through the swinging double doors and entered the Monitor Systems Control Room, the brain center of Water and Power. As usual, every phone in the place was ringing off the hook as the tech guys ran around like wild apes, struggling to keep up with it all. A few years back, Harry had offered Pete the opportunity — along with a substantial raise — to join the gang in MSCR. He'd almost panicked and fled the building, so terrified was he of ending up scrambling around in there with the rest of the sad sack technicians. Besides that, being stuck in MSCR would've made it a lot harder for him when it came time for lunch. Not surprisingly, Harry seemed very understanding of Pete's desire to remain in the field.

Speaking of the man in charge, Pete finally spotted him, bent over a computer monitor and looking only slightly more vexed than usual. Harry Kuhn's neatly-pruned gray hair and the electric cigarette dangling from his grizzled lips gave him the look of a 1960s-era NASA Mission Control Specialist.

"Hey, Harry," Pete said, approaching the bossman's station. "You got a second?"

Harry continued to squint at the monitor. "Make it quick — we got some vandalism on the line over in Valley Village and shit's balled up from hell to breakfast."

"I've had some, uh, personal issues come up," Pete said. "I was wonderin' if I could have a week off."

"Starting when? And please don't say tonight."

"No, no — I was thinkin' tomorrow. I wouldn't ask, but —"

Harry looked up from the monitor, scrutinizing Pete as if he were some sort of technical error that could be sorted out with a little re-routing and a donut or two. "You been working here for ten years and never missed a day. This serious? I mean, you need anything?

"Just the time off," Pete said, withering a bit under Harry's probing gaze.

"Take it," Harry said, his eyes returning to the monitor and the Valley Village troubles. "And call me if you need anything else."

"Thanks, Harry." Pete boogied on out of there while the boogieing was good. He didn't want to have to answer any more questions than he already had.

Harry's eyes flicked from his monitor to the swinging doors as Pete exited. "I swear that guy never gets any older," he muttered to no one in particular, the electric cigarette bobbing up and down between his lips.

13

Great. Now in addition to being scared shitless, Pete was wracked with guilt. He had gone into Monitor Systems Control fully intending to quit his job, but when he was face to face with Harry and all the hassles the poor guy dealt with on a daily basis, he couldn't bring himself to leave him hanging. *A week off.* Who was he kidding? Now he'd still wind up leaving Harry in the lurch, but he was gonna have to do it by phoning in from whatever corner of the world he crawled into in an attempt to hide from Carson Fitzgerald.

Pete had hoped to lay low for the rest of his shift, maybe even sneak back to his apartment and start packing, but within minutes of leaving DWP, he was called in to help with that vandalism issue in Valley Village. Whoever had caused it managed to create one spectacular clusterfuck, probably intending to shut down power to nearby businesses in hopes of an alarm-free crime spree, not realizing the security systems had backup power supplies. By the time the field techs had it buttoned up, Pete had to drive like a maniac to get home before sunrise. To make matters worse, he couldn't find a parking space within two blocks of his apartment building and had to run for home.

The sun's reddish glow was beginning to cut through the haze as Pete sprinted up the hill towards his building. Jumping a hedge, he cut across the lawn, huffing and puffing as he closed in on the front door. As he made to bound up the steps, something very much like an invisible shovel slammed into his face, sending him staggering back, disoriented and out of breath.

Teetering, Pete bent forward, hands on knees, fighting to stay on his feet. What the hell had he run into? Peering into the darkness, he spotted something at the base of the steps.

A goddamn *garden hose*, the water flowing across the ground past the bottom of the steps.

From the bushes, old man Stovall cackled gleefully. "You shall not pass, malevolent spirit," the codger croaked.

"Look, Gandalf," Pete wheezed. "I'm really not as malevolent as all that."

Mr. Stovall pointed towards the smoggy orange radiance

sliding into the sky in the east. "Your doom approaches!"

Regaining his composure somewhat, Pete straightened, sighing. "You've gotta lay off the horror movies, Mr. Stovall."

The old man watched in stunned silence as Pete approached the flow of running water from the garden hose, dodged to the right — away from the nozzle — then simply stepped over the hose. Pete shot him a look as he entered the building.

Glumly, Mr. Stovall shuffled over to the faucet and shut off the hose. He took a moment to enjoy the sunrise, then wandered off back to his apartment for some breakfast.

* * *

Since sleeping was unlikely on a good day, Pete figured it was pointless to even give it a shot under current circumstances. Instead, he dove into the horror of his closet and began sorting through clothes and other junk in preparation to flee the city. He still had no idea where he'd go — to be honest, he hadn't given it any thought; he only knew that he had to get the hell out of there and hope that Fitzgerald would be satisfied with dining on the vampires from Club Emoglobin. What the hell could've gone wrong with the guy's insides that caused him to have to drink the blood of other vampires, anyway? And more importantly, was it going to happen to Pete somewhere down the road? The thought of sinking his teeth into Bertrand Flagellamond's sickly-pale throat and sucking away at him like a big, bloody smoothie made Pete want to throw up even more than he already had that evening. The guy probably tasted like hipster douche when he was alive — Pete could only imagine how crappy the flavor had to be now that Bertrand was way past his expiration date.

On his knees in front of his jam-packed closet, Pete tried to put the thought out of his head and concentrate on the task at hand. He tugged a small wad of t-shirts from the heap, peeling them apart until he came to a pair that wouldn't give. Closer inspection revealed the shirts were glued to one another with something that looked like old pancake syrup. *Best not to delve any deeper*, Pete thought, flinging the Siamese twins into the trash pile. A damn shame, too — one of them was his beloved *Keep on Truckin'* shirt.

Needing further distraction, Pete shoved himself to his feet with the now-standard groan and walked to the bedside table, where he switched on the old clock radio. *Metal Guru* by T. Rex boomed from the tiny speaker, courtesy of the local classic rock station. Just the right kind of loud to put a fella at ease, even if he *was* about to skip town to avoid having his blood ingested by a sinister vampire.

Pete turned back towards the closet, eyeballing the shirts he'd extracted from the jumble. What was he gonna wear for his date with Angie? And why the hell was he still seriously considering showing up for that date, anyway? He peered into the depths of the closet, hoping to find something that might pass for fancy duds. The corner of something red and leathery caught his eye; he grabbed hold of it and yanked, spilling out an assortment of shredded jeans, more t-shirts, an old leather jacket missing one sleeve, and the floppy leather hippie hat he'd worn once (somewhere around 1968) before being overcome with embarrassment. He held up the object he'd pulled loose: an '80s-era jacket with ridiculous, pointy shoulders and the garish design of a rejected X-Men costume. *Ugh* — the eighties. What had everyone been thinking, anyway? Yeah, there were a lot of goofy outfits in the seventies, but if there was anyone alive who truly felt the fashions — or the music, for that matter — of the eighties were superior to *anything* from the seventies, Pete figured he could overlook his vow to feed strictly on goats and just suck down that goofball's blood, because it wasn't doing *him* any good. As Pete examined the horrendous jacket, he decided it was more Legion of Super-Heroes than X-Men — but only suitable for the most embarrassing member of the Legion, more *Tremendous Asshole Lad* or *Thompson Twin Boy* than Matter-Eater Lad or Mon-El. Disgusted with himself for ever having been fool enough to purchase the thing, he flung it into the trash pile, atop the sticky *Keep on Truckin'* shirt.

God damn that Carson Fitzgerald, anyway. This situation with Angie — she *dug* Pete, at least enough to sacrifice an evening of her time to decide if he was worth more of it, and if that British touch-hole hadn't reared his suave, pointy-toothed head back here in Los Angeles, Pete probably would've had a shot with the girl. Maybe. If he could just remember how to interact with another person without fainting and/or vomiting.

Screw Fitzgerald: Pete was goin' out on the town. He'd flee the country *after* his big date.

14

Pete cautiously opened the front door of the apartment building, peeking out to see if old man Stovall might be lying in wait. No sign of him, but the crotchety bastard could be hiding in the bushes, ready to leap out and cause more trouble for Pete — and Pete was a man who was pretty well fed up with trouble.

Feeling reasonably confident that Mr. Stovall must be napping or watching *Wheel of Fortune*, Pete slipped out, quietly pulling the door shut behind him. He had settled on an old Who tour shirt that didn't smell too bad and only bore one small hole, just under the right arm. It was a little more snug around his belly than he'd like, but as long as he didn't raise his arms over his head, his gut would probably remain concealed. Since his options for pants were limited to jeans, jeans, or shabbier jeans, he opted for his nicest pair, along with his work boots. Pete knew he was pretty damn far from snappy, but it was the best he could do. In his left hand, he carried a small hard-shell suitcase, crammed full of the few items he thought important enough to take with him when he split the scene after dinner with Angie.

At the sidewalk, he paused, looking up and down the street. Where the hell was his truck? Finally remembering he'd had to park a couple blocks over, Pete took it on the heel-and-toe. Nervously, he checked his watch — he was running a bit late and having to hoof it to the truck was going to add to that, especially if traffic was bad in Holly-wood.

"Pete!"

He nearly jumped out of his socks, his head frantically whipping back and forth. He relaxed somewhat as Pinball stepped out from behind a row of shrubbery. The big vampire girl appeared more than a little nervous herself, something Pete had never witnessed before.

"Holy shit," he said. "You nearly gave me a freakin'

heart attack."

"You're a vampire — you can't have a heart attack."

Pete glanced back towards his apartment building. "Keep it quiet, willya? I've already got enough problems with cranky ol' Van Helsing on the second floor."

"You've got a neighbor who knows you're a vampire and you haven't killed him?" Pinball shook her head. "No wonder you eat goats."

"I don't eat goats, I just… snack on them." Pete started walking again, faster this time.

Pinball hustled to catch up to him, eyeing his shabby suitcase. "So you really are leaving?"

Pete turned the corner. Pinball cut across the grass, coming up alongside him. "I've got somethin' to do, but yeah, after that I'm outta here. If you were smart, you'd do the same thing."

"That's what I need to talk to you about," Pinball said. Pete didn't respond. "Can you stop for a second? Jesus."

"Tell your story walkin'," Pete said, not looking at her.

Neither one of them noticed the large rat scurrying along behind them, ducking in and out of cover as it tracked the two vampires down the sidewalk. The creature's red eyes shimmered occasionally in the glow of the streetlights.

"Carmella and Bertrand and the others, they act like Fitzgerald isn't really a threat," Pinball said, nearly trotting to keep up with Pete. "Like they're his equals or something."

Pete elbow-checked Pinball — gently, so as to avoid an ass-kicking — to steer her through a left turn at the next corner. "Yeah, well, I got news for ya — they're not."

The rat scuffled beneath a hedge, slithering through the leaves and poking its head out the other side just as Pete and Pinball approached Pete's truck, parked at the curb.

"Fitzgerald didn't turn all of us so we could be some kind of vampire Round Table, hangin' out with him and swappin' stories about vampire shit." Pete pulled his keys, unlocking one of the large tool boxes on the truck's side. "He turned us because he wants slaves." He tossed his suitcase into the box and slammed the box shut, causing Pinball to jerk slightly. The big chick was scared, that was for sure. "If we don't perform that function well enough, he'll kill us. I've seen it happen and it ain't pretty. And now that he needs us for food, the slave option is an even worse deal, in my book."

Pinball absorbed this, her usual tough-chick demeanor replaced by a mask of worry.

"Why are you here, anyway?" Pete asked. "You don't even like me."

Pinball hesitated. "I wanna go with you. When you leave."

In the bushes, the rat listened intently.

Pete stared at her. How the hell was *that* gonna work? A hundred miles down the road and she'd be wanting him to pull over at a rest stop so she could drain the blood of some poor guy who just wanted to take a leak. Still, he wouldn't feel right leaving her behind — for one thing, she was the only one of the other vampires he didn't entirely dislike. And he wouldn't wish Fitzgerald on any of 'em, even Bertrand. "If I take you with me, we're not listening to any of that damn Goth dance shit."

Pinball perked up a bit. "I also like Tom Jones."

"Who doesn't?" Pete walked around the truck, opening the driver's door. "Where should I pick you up?"

"Outside the club, after closing. Say, three AM?"

"Okay." Pete got in the truck, slammed the door, and

fired up the engine. As he put it in gear, he stuck his head out the window. "You watch your back."

Pinball nodded, pleased. She watched as Pete drove away, turning the corner and disappearing from view.

Hidden in shadow, the rat's glittering red eyes followed Pinball as she walked off down the sidewalk.

15

Miraculously, Pete found a parking space on Sunset Boulevard right outside The Starbucket and was now hunkered down behind the steering wheel of the truck, fretfully staring at the bar. About fifteen minutes earlier, he'd been struck by the realization that he hadn't been on a date since 1973, and now he was — quite frankly — more frightened of walking in there and taking the girl out for dinner than he was of winding up a permanent blood-dispenser in Carson Fitzgerald's basement soda fountain of doom.

Across the street, the Goth-monkeys were beginning to line up outside Club Emoglobin. Francois le Sanguine held court amidst a small group of the nocturnal nerds, flamboyantly Anne Rice-ing it up in his frilliest vampire frock, a clove cigarette delicately cradled between his thin fingers. Pete considered running across the street and slugging the former Matt Stevens of Reseda right in his black and pouty kisser, but figured that was only a cheap delaying tactic. Time to man the hell up. Opening the truck's door, he got out and headed for The Starbucket.

Planted on a barstool with her back to the door, Angie

didn't see Pete enter the bar. Alvin Stardust was crooning *Red Dress* from the Starbucket's jukebox, doing a fair job of describing Angie's outfit — red pencil skirt hugging her shapely gams, black tank top, and a pair of wicked high-heeled Doc Martens boots.

Suzanne, serving as both waitress and bartender for the night, gestured with a disdainful jerk of her head. "Mr. Wonderful's here. It ain't too late to duck out the back."

"Put a sock in it," Angie said, swiveling her stool to get a look at her young man.

"Hey, it's your good time," Suzanne sneered.

Pete nervously approached Angie, taking stock of her sharp clothing. "I guess I already blew it," he said, awkwardly thrusting his arms out, drawing even more attention to his old t-shirt and inadvertently displaying the hole under the right arm.

"Don't sweat it," Angie said. "I like a man with a complete lack of style."

"He's got a style, all right," Suzanne interjected. "I call it *bum*."

"I thought I told you to shut up." Angie grabbed her purse off the counter as Suzanne *hmmf*ed loudly. "Don't mind her," Angie said to Pete. "You'd have to have a flaming skull tattooed on your face before you'd meet with her approval."

*Hmmf*ing once more, Suzanne threw in a dismissive cock of her hip to impart the colossal magnitude of her disapproval.

"Let's hit it." Angie thrust her hand into Pete's, causing goosebumps to squirm their way up his arm.

Suzanne's well-practiced scowl followed them all the way out the door. "Don't say I didn't warn you," she muttered.

In truth, Suzanne blamed herself for this dating debacle. As far as she knew, Angie's only social interactions were her shifts at The Starbucket, and with its clientele consisting of screenwriters and other losers, it's no wonder the girl would eventually settle for one of them. If Suzanne were any kind of a real friend, she would've been more aggressive in dragging Angie out to the right clubs, where she could meet the right kind of guy, instead of that dumpy construction worker or whatever he was. But maybe it wasn't too late — even if Angie went all moon-eyed over Mr. Chubbington, surely it would only take one night out on the town with Suzanne for her to realize she could do a hell of a lot better. Sure, Angie wasn't as hot as Suzanne and her friends — well, okay, as hot as *Suzanne* — but she was no embarrassment, either. She could land herself a bad boy, no problem — if she were willing to follow Suzanne's heartfelt guidance, of course. She could even think of one or two guys who might be willing to show Angie what she was missing.

Yeah… she'd have to get on this, maybe even make a few phone calls before the night was out. After all, it would be unfair of her to allow Angie to wind up in — *yuck!* — a *relationship* with the sort of dude who'd hang out in The Starbucket.

* * *

Pinball was walking out the door of Club Emoglobin when she spotted Pete and some chick leaving that shitty bar across the street. *What in the hell was that about?* Pinball stared on, bewildered, as Pete opened the passenger door of his truck for the girl. *A date?* Surely not, especially if Pete was really planning to skip town, and it seemed a safe bet he wasn't going to sink his teeth into her throat. For some reason, Pinball felt compelled to hide behind the first few people in line outside the club, spying on Pete from the safety of her Goth duck-blind. The big idiot was grinning so hard at the chick sitting in his truck, he almost stepped out in front of an oncoming car. Pete wildly leapt out of the way, arms flailing, then shot an embarrassed look at the girl. This time being a bit more cautious, he ambled over to the driver's door of the truck and got in.

What a mysterious sonofabitch that guy was.

"Pinball — did you hear what I said? Pull your head out of your ass."

Snapping out of it, she turned toward Bertrand Flagellamond, who was leaning against the wall with Francois le Sanguine. A pair of too-young club-girl acolytes stood nearby, basking in the radiant darkness of the two vampires, not realizing the trouble they were potentially setting themselves up for.

"Head up *what?*" Pinball said, irritated. She glanced back at Pete's truck just in time to see it drive off down Sunset. *Dammit.* Whatever he was up to, he'd better get his ass back in time to pick her up.

Bertrand held up two fingers. Francois obediently handed off his clove cigarette and Bertrand delicately slid the butt between his pursed lips, gazing at Pinball as he inhaled. "Walk with me," he said, letting the smoke trickle out along with his words. Leaving Francois and the club-girls behind, he stepped away from the wall and started down the sidewalk away from the club, gesturing for Pinball to join him.

She followed, not really wanting to have this conversation. When they were out of earshot of the crowd, Bertrand paused, looking past Pinball at Francois and the two girls. "Look at him — undead barely a month and he acts like he's some kind of dark lord of smooth."

"Did you bring me over here to bitch about Francois? 'Cause I've got shit I could be doing."

Bertrand continued to stare at Francois. "And you haven't been doing any of it, not since the idiot told us about Fitzgerald being back."

"He's not an idiot."

Bertrand cocked a neatly-plucked eyebrow.

"At least he's got the sense to get the hell out of town," Pinball said. "The rest of you are acting like it's no big deal."

"I wouldn't say that." Bertrand smiled at Pinball, as if trying to reassure a child. "We're all vampires. We just need to sit down with Fitzgerald, make him understand that he's been gone a long time — that things have changed."

Now it was Pinball's turn to raise an eyebrow. "Good luck with that."

Bertrand draped an arm across Pinball's muscular shoulders, guiding her back towards the club. "It's not like Fitzgerald's gonna burst into the club like the Terminator — he needs us. We've got all the bargaining power."

"I'm not sure I believe that," Pinball said, peeling away from Bertrand as they approached Francois and the adoring Goth girls.

"Loosen up," Bertrand said, eyeing the girls predatorily. "Enjoy the buffet."

Unconvinced, Pinball entered the club, hoping Pete would live up to his promise.

* * *

On Gower Street near Sunset Boulevard, Pete and Angie stood around with the other dozen or so people outside Roscoe's Chicken and Waffles, waiting for tables to open up in the restaurant. When they first arrived, Pete had spent a few uncomfortable moments fighting down the belief that everyone was looking at Angie and wondering what the hell she was doing with a schlub like him, but whenever she smiled at him, pretty much every thought in his head went right out the window, and she was smiling at him *a lot*, so he got over that bullshit in record time.

"You sure this is where you wanna eat?" Pete asked, secretly impressed that Angie had chosen Roscoe's as her ideal dinner-date destination. He was a bit concerned as to how he'd slide by the whole ordering-food-and-not-eating-it thing, but he was a firm believer in baby steps.

"Hell yeah," Angie said. "I'm gonna have the Scoe's Special and a Sunrise, with a big ol' slice of sweet potato pie for dessert." She rubbed her tummy in anticipation.

Pete smiled broadly. "Where you gonna put all that?"

"It's goin' straight to the ass, baby — straight to the ass."

Pete felt his face go all hot. Fortunately, at that precise moment, the host at Roscoe's banged the door open and called Pete's name, preventing Angie from noticing that her rather pale date had turned bright pink.

* * *

Suzanne wrestled the lid off a jar of maraschino cherries, dumping the contents into their slot in the plastic fruit tray holding olives, limes, and other garnishes for drinks requiring such things. Nazareth's *Hair of the Dog* erupted from the jukebox, flooding the bar with Dan McCafferty's snarling vocal and inspiring Suzanne to sing along with the chorus: "Now you're messin' with... *a son of a bitch!*" she howled, drawing nervous looks from the group of low-rent filmmakers parked at a corner booth.

After giving it some careful thought, Suzanne had settled on just the guy to set Angie up with — her buddy Korby. Not only was he the bass player for a smokin' hot band, he was an artist — sensitive, creative, and totally easy on the eyes, what with his tats and dreadlocks. As soon as she finished with the usual beginning-of-shift chores, she'd give him a call and see when he might be available to throw his goodness Angie's way. One night out with Korby and Angie would forget all about the boring chubster.

Suzanne flipped the lids closed on the fruit tray and took stock of the situation. Aside from the loser filmmakers in the corner, there was only one other customer in the joint —

Waitaminnit.

A layer of haze hung in the air, drifting slowly through the bar. *Some asshole was smoking.* The last thing she needed was to get cited because one of these jerks decided to sneak a ciggy on her shift. Suzanne turned her fierce scowl upon the table full of filmmakers, looking for the criminal in question. They all looked furtive but that was normal for them — they'd been regulars the entire time Suzanne had worked at The Starbucket, and they were all too chickenshit to try something like that, anyway. She turned her withering gaze upon the other customer, the sad-looking dude alone at a table near the trivia machine. Nope. Then where the hell was the smoke coming from? *Christ, please don't let the place be on fire*, Suzanne thought.

Turning, she was startled to find a new customer seated at the bar directly in front of her. He must have slipped in

unnoticed under cover of the raucous music. Good-lookin'
guy, too. Suzanne even managed to work up something
approximating a smile for the handsome devil. "What can I
getcha?" she asked, leaning forward just enough to give the
man a peek at her admittedly-spectacular cleavage. Tips, one
must remember, are very important to bartenders and wait-
resses. Distracted by the new arrival, Suzanne didn't notice
that the smoke cloud had disappeared entirely.

"I'm not sure," Carson Fitzgerald said, smiling wryly.
"What do you have on tap?"

16

The dinnertime racket at Roscoe's was a mix of clatter and
drone; excited voices and the sound of plates clacking
together or against tabletops as diners received their meals.
In one corner, gigantic actor Tiny Lister sat by himself,
overwhelming his table as if he'd been seated at a child's tea
party instead of a full-size booth. Watching the huge man eat
was a truly impressive sight, but for Pete, it was nothing
compared to seeing Angie tuck into her Scoe's Special. The
Scoe's consisted of a quarter of a fried chicken (Angie had
opted to have hers smothered in gravy and onions) and two
waffles. Nearly half of it was gone already, and the food had
only arrived at the table moments earlier. Pete had ordered
The Stubby, a fried chicken breast and leg, served up with a
side of grits, two eggs, and a biscuit. It remained, needless to
say, untouched as he stared at Angie.

Chomping away at a bite of chicken, Angie narrowed

her eyes at Pete. "Whatta you lookin' at?"

"I dunno," Pete said, somewhat abashed. "I just — I've never seen anything like this. Except at the zoo."

Angie gave him the stink-eye. "You callin' me a monkey?"

"The monkeys are dainty."

"Charmer. Just wait till the pie gets here." She waggled a chicken leg in the general direction of his plate. "At least I'm eatin'. You back on that screwy diet?"

Yipes. Here we go. Pete pushed at his grits with his fork, swirling the melting butter around. "I guess I'm a little distracted."

"Yeah, well, you'd best be gettin' focused and dig into that Stubby, or I'm comin' over the table after it," Angie said around a mouthful of waffle. Her eyes rolled upwards. "Holy crap, these waffles are good."

What Pete wouldn't give to find out just how tasty those waffles were. He looked at the food on his plate, feeling the twinge in his belly. He hadn't fed in a couple of days now, and puking three hundred times after having a bite of that cheeseburger the night before hadn't helped any. He wanted to shovel those grits into his mouth and pack them in with a fistful of chicken, but he knew that'd send him fleeing to the restroom to heave uncontrollably for another half-hour. Better to come up with some kind of lame explanation as to why he wasn't eating.

Ready to make with the bullshit, Pete looked up at Angie just as she crammed another forkful of waffle into her mouth. He stared blissfully at the sight.

Angie's chewing slowed, an embarrassed look spreading across her face. "Whaaaaat," she said, her voice muffled by the food.

The moment hung there as if Pete's world had suddenly gone into slow motion, the background din fading out of existence, every bit of his attention focused on Angie as Pete became well and truly aware of his good fortune. He didn't know what the hell Angie saw in him, but he was more than certain that this was the best night of his undead life — and the life before that, too. "You look... *great*," he said, very softly, like the air had gone out of him.

Angie's eyebrows wriggled toward each other as she appraised Pete, suspicious and uncharacteristically a bit off-guard. "Whatta you…" she began, realizing her mouth was still overstuffed with waffle. Chewing quickly, she swallow-ed and continued. "Don't make fun."

Pete shook his head. "I'm not —"

"Pssh." Angie interrupted, looking down at her plate, strangely demure.

"— making fun," Pete finished. "You're gorgeous."

She looked up at him again. "I'm covered with chicken grease."

Pete smiled. "Yeah. It kinda makes you sparkle."

"You're kind of a doofus."

"Yes," Pete said.

"And you're not gonna eat those grits, are you?"

"Probably not."

"You gonna take 'em home?" Angie's fork was slowly moving towards Pete's plate.

"Have at 'em," Pete said.

Angie scooped up a forkful of the grits. "You're not gonna think less of me, are you?"

"Hell no," Pete insisted.

Growling playfully, Angie shoved the fork in her mouth. "Mmm. Your loss, buddy."

Pete gave some very serious thought to the notion that he might pass out from sheer delight. Which helps explain why he slipped up so very badly a moment later.

"How long you lived in L.A.?" Angie asked, digging her fork into Pete's grits once again.

Caught up in the moment, Pete completely forgot to fudge the truth. "Since about 1957," he said.

Hoo boy, Pete thought. *What in the hell did I just do?* He could feel an incredibly stupid grin freezing into his face as he watched confusion cloud Angie's expression.

"Say what now?" she asked, the fork held motionless above Pete's plate.

"What?"

"You said you've lived here since 1957."

Pete suddenly felt even more like he might pass out, but this time it wasn't from delight. In fact, for a few seconds, he considered faking a stroke or setting himself on fire.

He weakly cleared his throat. "What'd I say?" *Oh Christ, do the math, do the math, how the hell old am I supposed to be —* "Since about 1997. Yeah, that sounds about right. Right?" Wishing for an earthquake, Pete lifted his water glass to his lips, realized he couldn't drink the stuff, then faked it awkwardly, spilling a bit onto his shirt. As he wiped at the wet spot, he was well aware of Angie's laser-like gaze upon him.

"You okay?" she asked.

"Yeah!" Pete blurted. "Yes. Listen, whatta you wanna do after this?"

"I dunno, I hadn't really thought about it," Angie said.

"Crap." *I screwed it all up.* Pete set his water glass down with a loud *thunk*, this time spilling some on the table.

"Did you mean to say that out loud?" Angie asked.

"Not really," he said. His napkin seemed terrifically interesting all of a sudden. He poked and prodded at it, finally wadding it up into a little ball. Looking up at Angie's puzzled expression, he let out an odd little sigh.

"You don't have to be nervous with me, Pete," Angie said.

God, she was pretty. Maybe it was for the best that Fitzgerald showed up — Pete figured he was blowing it so badly with Angie, he would've had to skip town out of sheer embarrassment anyway.

When Angie reached across the table and took his hand, Pete realized he was shaking. "I'm sort of… out of practice at this stuff," he said.

"It's cool," she said.

Pete looked into those green eyes and honestly believed she meant it. "Okay. So..." His hand continued to shake, but it was no longer because of frustration and embarrassment. "...After we finish dinner, you wanna see somethin' really cool?"

Angie's eyes narrowed. "Whatta you got in mind?"

Pete smiled mischievously.

17

Suzanne lugged a heavy case of Rolling Rock out of the back room, whacking her elbow on the swinging metal door in the process. "*Fuu-eckkk,*" she hissed through her teeth. At least she didn't drop the beer — that would've been a disaster, and probably would've come out of her paycheck, to boot.

She limped the case of beer over to the cooler mounted under the bar and struggled it down to the floor. Straightening, she exhaled sharply and prodded at the sore spot on her elbow.

The good-looking guy was still seated at the bar, but as far as Suzanne could tell, he hadn't even touched his drink. Figures. Showing a guy a little boob action didn't seem to count for much anymore, at least not in The Starbucket, what with the tight-fisted clientele. The lonesome loser had split, leaving but a few coins on his table, and the filmmaker geeks were in the midst of shoving their glasses up on their noses and brushing off their stylish dork blazers in preparation for what would no doubt be an exciting evening at the NuArt Theater for a double-feature of some shitty French flicks. At least those guys were usually good for a few bucks, probably figuring if they tipped something decent they might have a shot at getting into Suzanne's pants. *Call me when the box office numbers come in for your next hit, boys.*

Still, it was early, and The Starbucket stayed fairly consistent through the evening. And besides, Suzanne wouldn't mind if it stayed slow for an hour or so — playing both bartender and waitress had been more of a chore than she expected, and it would give her a chance to get caught up. Hell, even Larry the cook wasn't in yet — he'd called awhile back to tell Suzanne his car had broken down and he wasn't sure when he'd be there. This, by the way, was also perfectly fine with Suzanne, because Larry usually ended his shift by hitting on her, and his weirdly muscular forearms freaked her out. She could only imagine the disgusting things he did to build those particular muscles — she couldn't even eat the food at The Starbucket because of Larry's creepy forearms.

Worse yet — she hadn't had a chance to call Korby and see if he'd be willing to take Angie out and show her a proper good time.

Squatting down behind the bar, she busted open the flaps on the case of Rolling Rock and began stocking the cooler, the bottles clanking as she shoved them to the back. Hunkered down back there, something struck her as wrong. She froze for a moment, trying to figure out what it was.

Silence.

There was nothing on the jukebox. An odd occurrence in The Starbucket.

Unnerved, Suzanne tucked the bottle she was holding into the cooler, then stood, looking around the place. The filmmakers had left; the dude at the bar was the only customer remaining, and damned if his drink weren't still full.

"Looks like you're okay with that drink, huh, mister?"

"It'll do," Fitzgerald smiled. "For the moment."

Rapping on the bar in acknowledgement, Suzanne went to the register and thumbed a key to open it. The *ching!* seemed particularly loud in the quiet of the bar, the sound of the drawer banging open nearly making her jump. She fingered a few quarters out, shoved the drawer closed, and walked out from behind the bar, crossing to the jukebox.

Her face lit by the glow of the juke, she glanced back at the guy seated at the bar. If he wasn't gonna drink — and more importantly, *tip* — then maybe she could run him out of the place with a song nobody liked but her. Smirking with pleasure at the evil she was about to do, she dropped the quarters, punched a few buttons to line up a playlist sure to annoy, then headed back to the bar, glowering at the guy's back as he sat there not drinking.

She failed to notice that — despite being seated directly in front of it — he was nowhere to be seen in the mirror behind the bar.

The jukebox clicked and clunked as it brought up Suzanne's first selection. The bubblegum strains of Bobby Sherman singing *Easy Come, Easy Go* put an end to the uncomfortable silence in The Starbucket.

That oughta do it, Suzanne thought. Her love for *Easy Come, Easy Go* — and Bobby Sherman in general — was the subject of many cruel jokes amongst the bar's staff, but Suzanne didn't care. Her mom had played Bobby's records for her when she was a little girl, and she associated his songs with some pretty happy times.

As Suzanne passed the bar, she sneaked a peek at the dude, looking for any indication that the song was rattling his cage. She was annoyed to discover that he not only didn't appear to be on the verge of fleeing, he still had that tiny smile on his face.

Give it time, she thought. "I gotta get some stuff outta the back, mister," she said, cocking a thumb towards the swinging metal door. "Lemme know if you need anything, okay?"

The guy just nodded, still smiling. Maybe he was a closet Bobby Sherman fan.

Suzanne pushed through the metal door and into the back room, looking around for some sort of busy work she could futz through while waiting to see if *Easy Come, Easy Go* would have the desired effect. *Oh, hey — Korby*, she remembered. Pulling her cell phone from her pocket, she flipped it open and started going through numbers.

Behind her, she heard the metal door swing open, the

sound of Bobby Sherman's voice increasing in volume, then decreasing as the door swung shut again. Figuring it was Larry finally limping his way into work, she didn't give it much thought. "About time," she said. Her attention still on her phone, Suzanne turned, surprised to find Fitzgerald standing in the back room. She stared at him for a moment, confused. "You need somethin', mister?"

That smile tugged at the corners of Fitzgerald's mouth, but he said nothing.

Irritated, Suzanne lowered her cell phone. "You can't be back here, it's employees only."

Fitzgerald remained silent, his eyes focused on her. His head cocked to the side slightly, like a dog watching television.

"*Employees*," she reiterated. "If you need something you gotta go back up front and I'll be out there."

Still nothing. Suzanne was officially freaking out now. This guy was not normal. Maybe he was some kind of rapist or underpants freak or —

Oh Jesus, his eyes, what the hell is wrong with his eyes —

Black. His eyes had gone black, like a shark's eyes.

Cell phone. *Stupid, stupid*, it was in her damn hand, *call the cops* —

Suzanne raised the phone, went to stab the numbers.

Too fast to comprehend, Fitzgerald was on her, his hand closing over her mouth. Struggling wildly, Suzanne let out a muffled squeal as he lifted her a good ten inches off the floor. Her cell phone clattered to the concrete beneath her dangling feet, the display cracking.

His face close to hers, Fitzgerald's black eyes bored into Suzanne's. She watched in awe as his mouth opened wide, his fangs extending, running with saliva. Fitzgerald's free hand pressed against the small of her back, pulling her wriggling body closer to his own.

She gasped as the fangs punctured her throat, sinking into the flesh.

Groaning softly, Suzanne could hear Bobby Sherman singing to her as she drifted away from herself.

18

The sun was long gone, but the asphalt still radiated the heat of the day as Pete nervously took Angie's hand, leading her into the North Hollywood self-storage facility. It was one of those 24-hour coded entry places — popular with the sort of folks who run meth labs and don't want to cook the stuff at home; just rent a decent-sized storage room and set about producing your product. Pete had once met a struggling movie director who was secretly living in one of the smaller garages; the guy spent his days hanging out at DuPar's or Twain's, sucking down coffee, eating pancakes, and desperately trying to land a directing gig. At night he'd head back to the storage place, where he had a twin bed, a battery-powered camping light and the few other belongings he hadn't yet sold off. There was a short stretch of time where an editor buddy of the director's moved in with him, but in the confined space, the men quickly came to blows and the editor was forced to find other accommodations.

As he and Angie walked down a row of garages, Pete considered the possibility of moving into one of the places himself, if Mr. Stovall kept harassing him. It wasn't like he needed much in the way of apartment, but with his in-somnia, he figured he'd miss having cable TV. Probably got really hot in the summertime, too.

Angie squeezed his hand, rocketing a tiny thrill up Pete's back. "Is this the part of the date where you chop me into pieces and stuff me in a freezer?" she asked.

"Hatchet's in the truck," Pete said.

"Still, this is Los Angeles — you see it on the news all the time. Poor, unsuspecting girl goes off with a man she hardly knows, winds up in a shallow grave or a pot of soup…"

"I'm not a big fan of soup." Pete checked the numbers on the storage room doors, looking for the right one. It was at that unfortunate instant that his stomach took the op-portunity to yowl aggressively.

Angie stopped, her eyes widening. "Was that your stomach?"

"NO," Pete insisted. "Maybe."

"Little soup might do you some good," Angie said, patting his belly with her free hand and causing Pete to reflexively suck his chubby gut in slightly. "Seriously, I'm a little concerned about this screwy diet you're on. I haven't seen you eat anything except a bite of that cheeseburger the other night, then you ran out of the bar like the place was on fire."

Pete peered up the row of garages, pretending to be very intent upon finding the right one. "Yeah, I realized I was late for work. C'mon." Still gripping Angie's hand, he started moving again.

"It's not like you're fat or something," Angie pressed.

"Here it is," Pete said, happy to change the subject. Tugging his keyring out of his pocket, he walked Angie to the garage door. "Um…" He grinned at her, not wanting to let go of her hand, but needing both mitts to unlock the padlock on the door. To his surprise, rather than let go of his hand, Angie took the lock in her free hand, cocking it upwards so the keyhole was pointed at Pete.

"Stick it in," she said.

Pete felt his pasty face go all red once again. "Good Heavens."

"For a second I thought you said 'Good Heavens'," Angie mocked.

Feeling somehow naughty, Pete slid the key into the padlock.

"That's right, baby," Angie coaxed.

"Okay," Pete said, poised awkwardly at the lock. "You've gotta stop, you're killin' me."

"I'm just talkin' about padlocks." She smiled slyly at him. "Whatta you, got a dirty mind?"

Clearing his throat, Pete twisted the key in the lock.

"Ooo," Angie said as the padlock popped open.

"Hey now," Pete said.

Angie pulled the lock from the door, dropping it in Pete's hand. "All right — show me what you've got."

"Man, it never ends with you," Pete said, pocketing the lock and the keyring. Finally forced to release Angie's hand, he noticed with some embarrassment that his palm was sweaty. "You're gonna like this." Sliding the bolt back, he grabbed the handle and rolled the garage door up.

Angie peered into the dark storage room at a large *something* draped with a gray fabric cover. "Spectacular," she said. "Definitely worth the build-up."

"Wait for it." Pete entered the garage to stand next to the *something*. He waved his hands above the fabric cover with theatrical flair.

"All right, Criss Angel — make with the magic already."

Pete suddenly felt slightly panicked. *You're only making things harder*, he thought. *You're never gonna see her again after tonight*. Better to just cut this whole date business short. He stared at Angie's face for a very long moment, feeling himself sinking into those green eyes all over again.

Shut the hell up, he told himself.

Gripping the fabric cover, he quickly peeled it away from the *something* beneath — stirring up a massive cloud of dust in the process.

Coughing and waving her hands, Angie squinted through the dust at Pete's immaculate 1971 Plymouth Duster, the Sassy Grass Green paint job still looking factory-fresh. "Holy shit," she said, choking only a little.

"Yeah." Pete was still staring at Angie, the dust swirling around her, making her look like a tank-top-wearing angel emerging from a somewhat filthy cloud.

She stepped closer to him, her body bumping against his. Rather goofily, he felt his butt cheeks twitch momentarily. Angie took his hand, squeezing it. "You seriously better be plannin' on takin' me for a ride in that thing," she said.

19

Carson Fitzgerald drained the last drop of blood from the hapless jogger, the man's body going slack in the vampire's grip. Annoyed, Fitzgerald hurled the corpse into the bushes nearby. The jogger's bright red shorts stood out like an effeminate, butt-hugging beacon amidst the leafy branches, even in the darkness. Fitzgerald wasn't concerned about the body being found, but he needed a few more moments of privacy to carry the girl to his car — which is exactly what he'd been doing when the jogger came bounding down the road, eyes widening upon sight of the seemingly-lifeless woman in Fitzgerald's arms.

Idiots, these humans; wearing ridiculous outfits, trotting around at all hours of the day and night, sweating and huffing and gasping, all in a desperate — and ultimately pointless — attempt to prolong their lives. This particular jogger had only ended his that much sooner by choosing exercise over television and cheese doodles, or whatever garbage it was they liked to stuff themselves full of. Stepping towards the hedgerow, Fitzgerald shoved at the corpse with one foot, cramming it further into the vegetation. He squinted down at the body for a moment, aggravated that the red shorts could still be seen. Cocking back on one leg, Fitzgerald kicked the man directly in his red-clad rump, finally sinking him deep enough into the hedge to prevent him from being found for awhile.

Satisfied, Fitzgerald calmly strode back to the parked car he'd set the girl's body on when the jogger came upon them. This being Los Angeles, the act had set off the car's alarm, but — again, this being Los Angeles — no one seemed concerned by the noise. The whooping and shrieking of the alarm continued as Fitzgerald gathered the girl's limp form in his arms and continued walking up the street towards his own car, the little midnight-blue BMW Z4.

Fitzgerald couldn't remember the last time he'd been concerned about health or fitness, other than the need to avoid a self-styled vampire slayer now and again throughout the decades — although perhaps that fell into a different category. But with the sickness came something he hadn't felt in a very, very long time: *worry*.

And even, yes, a bit of fear.

He had no clue what had caused the sickness; he'd certainly never met another vampire who suffered from the malady. Was it age? Possibly some sort of virus? He'd spent plenty of time in some rather unsanitary locations while in Europe, after all. Still — if it *were* a virus, then it should have affected other vampires he'd met in his travels.

The girl stirred slightly in his arms, a soft moan escaping her bluish lips. Good. She was a strong one. She'd serve his needs well, then.

When the sickness first came upon him, Fitzgerald had assumed he simply needed to feed more often. It only took a few days and a dozen victims before he began to understand there was something terribly wrong with him, and by that time he'd racked up enough of a body count to draw the interest of the citizenry. And unlike the United States — where people are so (ahem) *sophisticated* you could turn into a bat in front of someone and they'd suggest you take that amazing act to Vegas — your average European was far more inclined to accept the notion that a vampire was gorging itself on the populace, and once they'd settled on that explanation, they dug out the garlic and sharpened the stakes without further discussion. Driven from the little German town where he'd been living, wandering sickly and weak through the countryside, Fitzgerald stumbled across another vampire: a young — well, using the term loosely — woman named Antje. She took him in, kept him safe, did her best to nurse him to some semblance of health without much

Scott S. Phillips

success, and early one morning when she returned from feeding, he repaid her kindness and hospitality by ripping her throat open. Antje clawed and kicked at him, fought like an animal, but as her thick blood flooded down his throat, Fitzgerald felt a strength he'd never known surge through him. He hadn't planned the attack; in fact, he'd embraced her lifeless body for a very long time afterwards, weeping and cursing himself and the sickness that drove him to it.

Up until that moment, Fitzgerald had never felt like a monster. But with the murder of Antje, he'd discovered the way to manage his illness.

When Fitzgerald began hunting — and killing — other vampires, he found himself pursued not just by men, but by his own kind as well. It was a terrible, solitary existence, hiding away rodent-like in the darkest holes, never mingling with vampire or human, skulking about in the shadows like some sort of madman.

Then he developed *the plan*.

Thin, pale, barely alive, Fitzgerald crept aboard a cargo ship, hiding away deep in its bowels, willing himself into a sort of hibernation. When the ship docked in New York, he awakened, crawling from the ship to slaughter three dock-workers and drink their blood. It was enough to keep him going. As he made his way across the country, he began taking what the horror movies would call his *vampire brides* — turning women, but in a way that left them simple minded, animalistic, easy to control. The blood of a recently-turned vampire didn't restore Fitzgerald to full strength, but it provided far more sustenance than mere human blood.

During his time away, Fitzgerald's home in Los Angeles had been maintained by his familiar, and the pitiful creature was overjoyed by the Master's return. Locked away in the

88

old house and feeding regularly on his brides, Fitzgerald slowly regained enough of his power to begin the final stages of his plan: gathering his children. The vampires he'd created over the decades would certainly provide the kind of blood he needed — he'd simply have to push himself away from the table before he drained them completely, then bring them human victims to restore their own blood, thereby insuring he'd have a steady supply of food.

First, however, he'd have to convince the others that it was in their best interests to serve his needs.

Reaching the BMW, Fitzgerald gently lowered the girl to her feet, leaning her against the side of the car and holding her up with one hand as he unlocked the passenger door. He'd gone to The Starbucket intending to visit the woman Pete Tyler appeared to have gone soft for, surprised when he found young Mr. Tyler apparently taking her out on the town. At first a bit concerned that he hadn't instilled the fear he'd hoped for in Pete and the others, Fitzgerald soon realized that the girl he'd bitten — this tattooed, ill-mannered hellion — would work even better for his purposes. He didn't want to crush Tyler completely; Fitzgerald still hoped that Pete might come around, even after all these years.

As for the others — they'd obviously grown arrogant in his absence and needed something more than gentle persuasion.

Opening the door, Fitzgerald lifted the girl once again, carefully placing her in the passenger seat and arranging her legs in a lady-like manner, knees together and towards the inside of the car. He shut the door, then looked down the road toward Sunset Boulevard. He couldn't see Club Emoglobin from his vantage point, but even over that damnable car alarm, he could hear the dreadful music the vampires there felt compelled to subject themselves to.

A tiny shudder of revulsion ran through Fitzgerald's body at the thought of entering the atrocious nightclub. Grateful he knew where his children lived, he walked around to the driver's side of the car, ready to carry out the rest of his evening's business.

20

Alice Cooper's *Wish I Were Born in Beverly Hills* pounded from the car's stereo speakers as Pete revved the Duster's powerful engine, eliciting a squeal of pleasure from Angie. They were currently stuck in traffic on Hollywood Boulevard, moving at the blistering pace of about five yards every three or four minutes, but they were both having a hell of a good time.

Whooping loudly, Angie pumped her fist out the window in time to the music. On the Walk of Fame, two skaterkids paused in scrounging for change long enough to flip her off. "Eat it, punkass bitches!" Angie hollered.

Pete goosed the engine again and the Duster rumbled magnificently as it inched along the road. "Chinese Theater," Pete said, pointing up ahead.

Angie stuck her head out the window, gawking at the famous movie palace. "Y'know, I've lived here a year and I've never even been on this street," she said.

"You've never been to Hollywood Boulevard? What the hell did you come to L.A. for?"

Angie settled back into her seat, suddenly pensive. "Vacation, kind of."

Pete looked at her, confused. "You're on vacation but you're working as a bartender?"

"Vacation's over," Angie said.

"I do believe there may be more to this story," Pete prodded. As they waited in traffic, his foot played the Duster's gas pedal up and down, creating a symphony of beautiful Detroit noise.

"Hey, it's not like I know anything about you. Except you have the coolest goddamn car I've ever seen."

Pete smiled. "Here's what I know about *you:* you went on vacation and got a job, you're a stone fox, and you have a talent for removing model car windshields from the fingers of idiots."

"I'm a stone fox?" That spectacular, kittenish grin played across Angie's face again. "Keep on truckin', dude."

Dammit, Pete cursed himself. *I need to get with the current lingo.* "You're def and fresh?" he tried.

"Whatever, Jazzy Jeff." Angie sucked in a deep breath, steeling herself. "I came out here on a sort of gettin' away from it all trip. Never used the return ticket."

"What were you gettin' away from?"

"See, this is why I said I was on vacation, I knew there'd be questions."

"Sorry," Pete said. "It's cool if you'd rather not talk about it."

"Aah, I guess it's all part of the uncomfortable-first-date thing." She looked at Pete, turning away again when he met her gaze. "I was comin' out of an ugly situation with a good-lookin' guy. The ugly kept happening even after I came out here, so I decided I wasn't goin' back."

"What was he, a cheatin' bastard?"

"On his good days."

The traffic light ahead went red and Pete rolled the Duster to a stop. He took the opportunity to stare at Angie for a few seconds, feeling like a class-a dickhead. "I'm sorry, I was just tryin' to —"

"Naw, it's cool. I'm not a big moper or somethin', what happened happened, and I'm well rid of it. The guy sucked." She glanced over at Pete's hand resting on the gear shift, then put her hand over his. "You don't."

If you only knew, Pete thought.

Trying to think of something to say, he noticed her looking past him, out the window on his side of the car.

"Is that guy wantin' to race?" she asked.

Pete turned to see a pompadoured rockabilly cat at the wheel of a primer-gray rat rod in the next lane, a big grin on his face and his greasy head continually bobbing towards the road. "Either that or he's narcoleptic," Pete said.

"Maybe he was attracted by your ancient slang." Angie playfully jabbed a finger into Pete's flabby side.

"Hey," Pete scolded, trying to pull his love handle away from her finger.

"Let's show him who's boss," Angie said.

How can you be so amazingly cool, Pete wondered, staring at Angie as if she'd just shot lasers from her eyes. He turned to the rockabilly cat again, cocked his head in the universal motorhead signal for *You're On*.

The light turned green. Pete jammed the gas pedal. Angie shrieked in excitement. The rockabilly cat muscled his own engine, lighting up the tires of the rat rod, and the race was on —

For the next 15 yards or so, where Pete and the

rockabilly cat found themselves once again stuck in Hollywood Boulevard traffic. Laughing, the hepcat shot Pete and Angie a thumbs-up. Delighted, Angie threw her arms around Pete, squeezing him tightly.

Pete had never been so happy in his entire life.

Even when the cop rolled up behind them, flashers lighting up the night.

* * *

The traffic ticket wasn't bad — it was hard for a fellow to drive too recklessly or speed too much when he only went 40 or 50 feet up the road. And it certainly wasn't enough to crunch Pete's buzz.

He'd become somewhat edgy when Angie suggested they go somewhere a little more private, however. Pete knew of a parking spot on Mulholland Drive with a great view of the city, but once he'd pulled the Duster off the road and killed the engine, it occurred to him how uncomfortably close they were to the place where Fitzgerald had come back into his life.

That wasn't what had him on edge, though.

"Man, I knew when you asked me if I wanted to see somethin' cool it was gonna end with me havin' to fight you off," Angie said.

Pete's eyes widened. "No — I'm not —" he practically yelped. "Um," he added suavely.

Angie leaned against the door, eyeing him with suspicion. "Then you're gonna have to fight *me* off, I guess." Flipping up the arm rest that separated their seats, she slid over towards him.

Pete recoiled in alarm, an odd little sound finding its

way from his throat.

Angie hesitated. "You okay?"

"Yeah, just…" Pete sighed, feeling quite the tool. It was like his first time all over again.

"Been awhile?"

Pete nodded. "You have no idea."

Shrugging, Angie slid closer to him. "It's like ridin' a bike." She snaked an arm behind his neck, her other hand on his thigh.

"I don't know how to ride a bike."

"Stop talking," Angie said.

Then, with Pete comfortably trapped against the driver's side door, Angie leaned in and kissed him. And while it was true he'd never ridden a bike in his life, some things just come naturally.

Even to a vampire.

21

Standing alone on the sidewalk outside Club Emoglobin, Pinball checked the time on her cell phone: 3:24 AM. Goddammit, as soon as she saw Pete leave The Starbucket with that chick, she had a feeling he was gonna leave her twisting. Calling him a goatsucker the other night may not have scored her any points, now that she thought about it. She probably should've been nicer to him all along — he was easier to talk to than most of the other vampires, but he could be such a dick sometimes, especially about music. She wouldn't have figured him for a guy who'd break a promise, though.

Sighing very softly, Pinball stepped to the curb, looking hopefully up and down Sunset Boulevard. The street was weirdly quiet at that hour, the clubs closed, their patrons having long since split for the after-hours joints or the all-night diners. Traffic was light, and there was no sign of Pete's truck heading her way.

And Pinball, frankly, was scared shitless.

The muscular vampire girl checked the time again. Two entire minutes had passed. Anxiously, she nibbled at her lower lip, her right fang prodding the soft flesh. That goatsucker thing, that was just friendly ball-busting. Pete knew that, right?

"There you are!"

Startled, Pinball whirled, half-crouching and ready to brawl, only to find Bertrand Flagellamond flouncing his way out of the club, a dull-looking goth girl tucked in the crook of his thin arm. "God damn it," Pinball snarled, her muscles uncoiling. "That's twice tonight, Bertrand."

"And what did I tell you earlier? Ass, pull head out of?"

The goth girl *tee-heed* stupidly. She looked to be barely legal, let alone of drinking age, but she held a nearly-empty bottle of Heineken in her hand, black lipstick smeared around the bottle's rim. Her smallish breasts were shoved violently upwards by her red Wonderbra, the false cleavage blossoming from her fishnet top.

"I didn't know anyone was still inside," Pinball said, pocketing her cell phone and trying to seem nonchalant.

"Just us twain." Bertrand rested his chin atop the goth girl's head. "I thought you might like to join the lovely Miss Jade Darkloin and myself... for a drrrrrink?" He punctuated this by slipping his head down to playfully chomp at the goth girl's neck. "Nom nom nom!"

Jade Darkloin giggled.

Pinball felt like throwing up. "Not tonight, thanks."

Bertrand pouted, then shrugged. "Ah well — more for me, then."

"More for *us*, you mean!" Miss Darkloin corrected, blissfully unaware of what she was getting into.

"Of course — silly me." With a hand on the girl's rump, Bertrand prodded her into motion, shooting a campy wink back at Pinball. "Sinister laugh!"

Okay, Pete was easier to talk to than *all* the other vampires.

Pinball watched as Bertrand and the girl strolled off down the sidewalk, turning at the corner and disappearing. She tried to remember exactly when it was Carson Fitzgerald had walked her off into the night in a similar fashion — 1985? Or was it '86? Jesus, you'd think you could pinpoint something like that down to the hour. She'd been naive, foolish, just like the goth girl — although not as young. Fitzgerald was like a rock star to her, charismatic, handsome, and just the right kind of dangerous. If she'd only known. Not one to go in for the tortured, mopey posturing so many of the other vampires defined themselves by, Pinball had embraced the lifestyle — and the power that came with it. The vampirism was the ultimate extension of the physical strength she strove for, an unstoppable outlet to express her rage. Before she was bitten, she'd always hung with the goth crowd, but unlike most of them, she spent her days in the gym, slinging the iron, learning to fight. Nights she spent in the clubs with her friends, but more often than not those nights ended with her brawling in an alley, desperately trying to prove —

What, exactly? What the hell had made her so angry? Pinball struggled to recall what it was that might have driven her so ferociously, and what had made Fitzgerald so appealing, as if being in his orbit could somehow supply whatever it was that had been missing from her life. The years before she was turned were only a blur of memory now, a weather-worn sign painted on an ancient brick wall. She couldn't remember ever giving much thought to the future in those days because it just didn't matter; now she wasn't sure she'd have one at all, and suddenly it was all she wanted.

With one last, forlorn look up and down Sunset Boulevard, Pinball wandered off down the sidewalk, unsure where she was going.

Crouched atop a building not far away, Carson Fitzgerald watched his children scatter in the night.

22

"This is Badfinger," Pete said.

Nestled against his chest, Angie lifted her head and looked at him as if he'd just offered to perform a particularly naughty act.

"The song — remember? I said your name was like the Badfinger song? This isn't the one I was thinking of, that's *Dear Angie*, but this is Badfinger." He gestured towards the radio, currently playing *No Matter What*, by the band in question.

"Really? I thought this was a Def Leppard song." Off

Pete's stunned expression, she quickly added "What, I don't know these things."

"Def Leppard," Pete said, flatly.

"Whatta you got against Def Leppard? Joe Elliott was a stone fox."

"It's a long walk back to your place," Pete said.

"You wouldn't do that. Not when we're havin' such a good time." Angie rested her head on his chest again.

Pete awkwardly cocked his head to look at her. "You're havin' a good time?"

"You *do* get smarter, right? I mean, as things go along?"

"Things are gonna go along?"

"Forget it, I think you just answered my question."

Pete was playing it up now, enjoying the back and forth. "I think this is as smart as I get. I could shoot for better-looking, if you want."

"Maybe a Joe Elliott haircut?"

"Doubt I could pull that off. Will you settle for a Jeff Lynne 'fro?"

"Who's Jeff Lynne?"

"Oh my God — outta the car."

"You think you're so cool —" Angie poked a finger into Pete's belly fat once again "—name the members of Korn."

"Nobody can name the members of Korn," Pete sneered.

"They sure can," Angie insisted. "*You* can't."

"Name two."

"Jonathan Davis."

"Okay," Pete said.

Angie hesitated, unable to come up with another member of the band.

"You know you could just rattle off a bunch of made-up names and I wouldn't know the difference, right?" Pete asked.

"See? You're uncool."

"Wait a minute, then so are you, you can't name 'em!"

"I am one-fourth cool. Officially." Angie punctuated her proclamation by rapping her fist in the center of the Duster's steering wheel, sending up a short bleat of the horn. "Let's go somewhere and watch the sunrise."

Oh SHIT.

In a near-panic, Pete fumbled his right arm from around Angie's warm body and checked his watch. "Jesus Christ, it's after four AM!" Practically shoving Angie off himself, he grabbed the key in the Duster's ignition and fired up the engine.

Confused, Angie watched Pete as he dropped the car into reverse and started backing it out of their parking spot. "Are you okay?"

"Yeah, I'm fine, I'm fine."

"You're all frantic all of a sudden, what's up?"

Pete struggled to come up with some kind of reasonable explanation for his behavior. He'd been so lost in Angie he'd forgotten about Pinball, Fitzgerald, even the goddamn sun. "Nothing, nothing — I mean, I've gotta get the Duster back into storage, get home — it's late, y'know?" He smoked the tires of the car only a little as he took off down Mulholland. Without even looking, he could sense Angie's bewildered, hurt expression as she settled back into the passenger seat, very far away from him. Not thinking clearly, Pete tried to look at his own miserable expression in the rear view mirror, but of course he saw nothing.

* * *

Angie rode in silence all the way back to The Starbucket, but there was plenty of noise going on inside Pete's fevered brain as he mentally beat the living hell out of himself for being such a complete dumbass. Not only had he acted the fool with Angie, now he was going to have to race the sun in order to get the Duster socked away and make it home before he went up like a chubby sparkler. Not to mention he'd have to postpone leaving town for another day.

"I'm parked up around the corner here," Angie said as they rolled up Sunset, towards the bar.

Pete was happy to have the uncomfortable silence broken, but Angie's voice had the sort of flat, dull tone that pretty much ensured she was as upset as he figured her to be. Wanting to say something but afraid he'd only make things worse by speaking, Pete wheeled the Duster around the corner and up the side street Angie had indicated.

"That's me — the crappy little blue car." Angie pointed at a battered Geo Metro parked up ahead.

Pete pulled up next to the Metro and dropped the Duster into park. He looked at Angie. She was staring at the car's dashboard. "I've got nothin' against Def Leppard," he finally said.

Angie looked at him, the tiniest hint of a smile at the corners of her mouth.

Encouraged, Pete continued. "They had a pretty thick guitar sound."

"You married?" Angie asked.

Taken aback, Pete stammered for a second before blurting out "Heck no."

Angie's eyes narrowed accusingly. "You sure about that?"

"I'm not married."

"You're actin' like a guy who's gotta get home to his wife before she starts thinkin' he mighta skipped out of work to fool around."

"No, no way. I promise."

She stared at him for a few moments. "Okay. You're sure acting weird, though."

"That's… kinda my thing," Pete said.

A massive wave of relief washed over Pete when she smiled at him. "Yeah, no kidding." She opened her door, then turned to look at Pete, who was opening the door on his side. "What are you doing?"

"Walking you to your car."

"It's like, two feet away."

"There could be werewolves."

Angie shook her head, amused, then stepped out of the car. Pete came around the front end to meet her at the door of her Metro. Still slightly hesitant, she tapped a finger against his chest. "I had a pretty freakin' great time tonight, even if you *are* a weirdo."

"Pretty freakin' great is good."

"Yeah." She leaned in to lay a big smooch on him, then stepped back to look into his eyes as if trying to sort out just what the hell might be going on in there. "I'm off tomorrow night — well, I guess it's tonight, technically. That's a hint, if you're not busy."

The close proximity of the girl was futzing with Pete's wiring and he spoke without thinking. "Yes please."

"Good answer." Unlocking the Metro, Angie tugged the door open, the world-weary metal creaking sourly. As she settled into the seat, she threw Pete the devil-horns. "Rock rock till you drop," she said, closing the door.

Angie's smooth exit was marred only a little by the

Metro's stubborn refusal to start, but after a few tries, the engine caught and Angie rattled the little car off down the road. Pete stood there watching until the Metro faded into the night.

Damn it, now he was gonna have that song stuck in his head for hours.

23

Bertrand Flagellamond, once known as Martin Peck, strutted vivaciously across the living room of his one-bedroom apartment and jabbed *play* on the stereo. The anguished wail of HIM's *Join Me in Death* filled the room, much to the delight of Jade Darkloin, currently sprawled on the red velvet Victorian-era couch. She was going for seductive, but her inexperience made her look more like a broken marionette tossed aside by a drunken puppeteer.

The apartment building where Bertrand lived was as much an affectation as everything else about the vampire; an art deco masterpiece rumored to have been the sight of many a wild debauch back in the glory days, circa 1930-1940, and definitely the sight of at least one murder. None of these events occurred specifically in our Mr. Peck's apartment, but no one needed to know that. Upon moving in, he'd outfitted the place in goth splendor, painting the walls crimson, purple and black, covering every available surface with candles and skulls and all manner of nether-worldly items.

In his previous life, Bertrand had been a rising superstar at a North Hollywood copy shop, a specialist in the art of making screenplay copies: three-hole punch was no problem for him, and he was well on his way to the coveted assistant manager position and a solid future. His co-workers and superiors were unaware that the young man tended to cry himself to sleep most nights, lonely and frustrated and quite seriously considering going on a store-wide murder spree, planning to take out as many of his fellow employees as possible, the frosting on the cake being the opportunity to remove a few aspiring screenwriters from the gene pool, as well. Martin Peck was a classic nebbish (albeit one with sociopathic tendencies and a deft hand with the image-adjustment button on most of your upscale copiers) — his unwashed mop of mousy-brown hair dangling down over his thick glasses, creating a nest of acne on his forehead; his thin frame draped with ill-fitting, fashion-unconscious clothing. The chicks, they did not dig him.

Then Carson Fitzgerald came into his life.

Depressed, half out of his mind, and marginally hungry, Martin had gone out late one night planning to buy a pawn-shop handgun; when he chickened out, he went into the Rite-Aid nearby and bought an ice cream cone instead. As he was making his way across the parking lot back to his car, Fitzgerald hit him like a shark taking a seal. He could still remember staring at the chocolate and vanilla swirl, upside down on the asphalt, as Fitzgerald's fangs punctured his throat.

Bertrand had no idea why Fitzgerald chose to turn him, or even simply to feast upon his feeble blood, but when he'd arisen as an undead creature of the night, he took to it with gusto. Figuring he'd look pretty silly romping around Hollywood in the wee hours while clad in his nerdy Martin Peck attire, he did some shopping at the trendy joints he'd always fantasized about entering, wrecking his savings account but stocking up on leather pants and mesh shirts. A hipster barber, a little hair dye and some pomade took care of his mop, and fortunately, vampirism seemed to be its own cure for acne. Add a bit of black lipstick and Bertrand Flagellamond was born.

He only wished the copy shop had been open nights; he would've gone through the place like a weed-eater in a box of hamsters.

Bertrand tried to friendly-up with Fitzgerald at first, but the older vampire had blown him off, not really wanting anything to do with him. Afraid he'd merely traded being a living social misfit for being an undead one, Bertrand soon discovered vampirism not only took care of zits, it gave him the ability to sway people to his desires, particularly if they were already inclined towards the dark and mysterious — and so Bertrand began hanging out in L.A.'s goth clubs, quickly learning the strangely undulating little dance the goth-types like to do. It was in one of these clubs that Bertrand met Carmella Crimsonella, owner of Club Emoglobin, and a more experienced vampire — the assistant manager of vampires, as Bertrand liked to think of her. Introducing him to the other vampires Fitzgerald had created and abandoned, Carmella helped Bertrand through the rough patch until his vampire training wheels came off and he was better able to handle himself in a dark-lord-of-the-night kind of way.

Leather pants, jet pompadour and vampiric powers of seduction aside, however, much of the time Bertrand still felt like the same old dork he'd been when he was just Martin Peck, and that feeling only increased once he heard Fitzgerald had returned. He tried to act like he wasn't concerned about the threat their master represented — it irritated him to see Pinball and Elric all in a twist over it — but deep down, Bertrand knew he was more afraid than any of them. His sociopathic urges kicking in, he'd begun plotting various ways in which he might get close enough to Fitzgerald to hammer a stake through the old bastard's black heart. If Bertrand could end Fitzgerald's reign, Carmella would naturally step into the manager position — to continue the copy shop metaphor that never seemed to leave Bertrand's thoughts — and he'd move up a notch in the hierarchy. Hell, killing Fitzgerald might even leapfrog Bertrand directly to the top of the heap.

But first, *dinner*. Bertrand eyed the young woman flung haphazardly across his couch, his tongue slithering hungrily across the tips of his fangs. Martin Peck certainly never could've lured a girl like that back to his shithole apartment in North Hollywood — sadly, Martin had never lured *any* girl back to his apartment, or even spoken to one much more than to ask how many copies she needed.

Being a vampire was good.

Bertrand casually strolled over to the couch and sprawled seductively — because really, would Bertrand Flagellamond sprawl any other way? — alongside Miss Darkloin. She giggled as the vampire nibbled at her pale and tempting flesh. Nuzzling her ear, he whispered ever-so-softly: "Are you prepared to take your first step into the world of darkness?"

"I'm pretty drunk," she slurred.

Bertrand gently scraped his fangs across her neck. "Then loose your shudders of playsure as I devour the crimson —"

"Did you say *playsure?*" Jade Darkloin interrupted, giggling once again.

Bertrand's face went hot as the nebbishy old Martin Peck came hurtling to the surface again, fueled by this idiotic little bitch's mockery. His phony attempts at seduction instantly wiped away, Martin — Bertrand, *Bertrand* — snarled angrily, fangs poised above the girl's pulsing jugular, ready to plunge into the soft meat and take what he wanted — not just her blood, but her stupid *life*, her taunting laughter, her barely-concealed disdain for the nerdy loser he knew she saw him as.

Shards of glass flew into the room as the French doors leading to the balcony burst inwards.

Bertrand knew what was happening before he even caught sight of the massive bat-thing hurtling through the doorway, already transforming into Carson Fitzgerald. A chill wind swirled through the room, extinguishing the dozens of candles and whipping Bertrand's hair as Fitzgerald slammed to the floor.

Jade Darkloin finally developed the sense to be scared, scrambling from beneath Bertrand and going over the back of the couch.

Bertrand stumbled to his feet as Fitzgerald strode the last few feet towards him. "I know my place, Master — I swear —"

Fitzgerald's hand shot out, grabbing Bertrand by his well-coiffed pompadour and lifting him off the floor. Bertrand shrieked in fear and pain. "Please —" he begged, a bit of spittle flying from his mouth to spatter Fitzgerald's cheek.

Sneering, Fitzgerald drew his knife, the gleaming blade catching Bertrand's wild gaze. He saw the knife move suddenly, felt the razored edge slash deeply into his throat. Hot liquid flooded down over his mesh shirt. With a brutal twist,

Fitzgerald tore through the remaining flesh and bone, pulling Bertrand's head completely away from his shoulders. The last thing Bertrand saw was the girl peering in horror over the back of the couch as his body slumped to the floor.

Fitzgerald carelessly flung Bertrand's head away, sending it hurtling through the balcony doors. There was a loud thump followed by the wail of a car alarm as the severed head bounced off a parked car, then rolled beneath the heavy shrubs lining the apartment building's grassy yard.

Jade Darkloin whimpered very quietly as Fitzgerald crouched next to Bertrand's body. The vampire looked up at the girl as if just noticing her. "Go home," he growled.

Not yet understanding just how fortunate she was, Miss Darkloin fled the apartment.

Fitzgerald drank deeply of his misbegotten child's rich blood, feeling the strength flow through his body like an electric current.

* * *

The morning sun beat down on the apartment building, now the scene of yet another grisly Hollywood murder. Numerous police cars lined the street, most of the cops searching the yard, while a few others looked down from Bertrand's balcony. For a crime involving a headless body, they were puzzled as to the significant lack of blood at the scene.

"Got it!" one of the cops announced as he peered beneath the thick shrubbery.

Photos were taken and evidence collected before the officer who'd made the discovery was tasked with the duty of extracting the head of Bertrand Flagellamond from its hiding place. Donning a rubber glove, the cop hunkered down and reached under the bushes, fumbling around until he got a hold of Bertrand's tousled hair. Dragging the severed head from the shrubs, the cop held it up for the others to see.

The officers on the scene were unable to explain the bizarre manner in which Bertrand's head suddenly flamed out like a marshmallow over a campfire, falling to ashes at the startled cop's feet.

24

She didn't like lying, but Angie figured it was easier to let Pete think she'd been slapped around by some wife-beatin' asshole than to tell him the truth about why she'd fled Brooklyn. That unpleasant conversation would have to come eventually, unless Pete kept freaking out and wound up dumping her, but it might go a little more smoothly if she could wriggle further into his affections before dropping the bomb.

Is that manipulative and bitchy? she wondered. No. Okay — manipulative, yes, bitchy, no. And maybe (she hoped) not even all that manipulative when it came right down to it. After all, it wasn't like she was hiding her spectacularly successful sex-change operation from Pete, or leading him on so she could get her hands on his fabulous wealth; she genuinely liked the guy and simply didn't want to scare him off with anything weird before he really got a chance to know her. Weird's a lot easier to accept when you like some-one.

Angie just hoped Pete already liked her enough to forgive a little stalking, which she was quite possibly en-gaged in at the moment. Glancing away from the traffic on Franklin Avenue, she checked the piece of paper she'd written Pete's address on, looking up just in time to hit the brakes and skid to a stop a few inches shy of rear-ending the SUV waiting to make a left turn. Angie managed to fight down the ingrained New Yorker response to such a situa-tion, going so far as to shove her hands under her thighs to avoid honking the horn and flipping off the driver of the SUV. She very quietly muttered a few choice expletives, however.

Showing up unannounced wasn't really stalking, either, dammit. Looking up a guy's address on the Internet was iffy, but if she'd been carrying a delicious Jell-O salad, nobody would see it as anything other than being neighborly. She was just being paranoid.

She was also hoping like hell that Pete's door wouldn't be opened by another woman.

Despite his assurances otherwise, Angie was still harboring the fear that Pete was, in fact, married. And if not, there was definitely something up that had caused him to go into full-blown flip-out mode during their date the previous night. This unexpected mid-afternoon visit to his apartment wasn't entirely meant to catch him in the act of...*whatever,* but she'd be lying if she said that weren't part of her reason for doing it.

Angie had dated one other guy besides Pete since moving to Los Angeles, and she'd been overjoyed when she found out *he* was married. And come to think of it, *dated* might be the wrong word for that relationship — *unsuccessfully avoided* was probably a better way to put it. Hollywood is a hard place to be lonely, and an even harder place to meet someone you'd actually want to spend your time with. Now and again the loneliness will win out over your better judgment and you find yourself involved with a fellow like Johnny Jerkov.

"Jerkoff?" Angie had asked when the man finally walked over to her table and introduced himself. She'd been spending her mornings at a little coffee house on Highland Avenue, mostly to avoid her trio of roommates as much as possible, and she'd caught the not-unattractive fellow eyeing her on a good number of those mornings.

"Kov, JerKOV," Johnny replied, obviously used to hearing it. An old Polish name, he claimed. Mr. Jerkov skated the razor's edge between scruffily handsome and hipster douche, but his face was intriguingly rugged enough that Angie was willing to give him the benefit of the doubt. She was fairly certain the stylish rips in his jeans came from the factory rather than wear, and his pocket tees were always a bit too snug for her taste — she didn't really like a guy to have nipple bumps; it was unpleasant for everyone on the planet and no doubt led to hushed chatter amongst those in the general vicinity. Still and all, though — lonely she was, and it wouldn't hurt to at least make a friend.

They talked over coffee for the better part of an hour, until Johnny had to leave for an appointment, scribbling his number on a napkin and asking Angie for hers. She wasn't all that interested in the guy — for one thing, he constantly peppered their conversation with thinly-veiled double-entendre, and whenever Angie called him on it, he played annoyingly dumb — but she gave him her number anyway, figuring she might hang out with him at least once more, see if he had any interesting friends.

He called her two hours later, asking for a ride home from that appointment. Caught off-guard, Angie agreed to pick him up, only realizing as she was driving through Van Nuys that she should've told him to take a bus. She'd whipped herself into a fairly righteous fury by the time she arrived at the nondescript warehouse center where Johnny stood waiting for his ride, but somehow the sight of his big, handsome smile had a soothing effect on her, and — puzzled by the words she heard spilling from her own mouth — she found herself apologizing for traffic being so bad.

Angie wasn't the sort to be swayed by a pretty face, so she had a difficult time understanding the way things transpired after that. Following a couple more instances of giving him rides and/or running into him in various places, there was no doubt in her mind that Johnny was a nitwit, albeit a relatively harmless and even sort of charming one, and she'd be better off staying away from the guy. Somehow, though, as much as she tried to keep Johnny at a distance, she kept getting sucked into his gravitational pull without ever actually entering the atmosphere, so to speak. The entire time she was "dating" him, he never made a move on her, and while she certainly wasn't interested in taking a grab at the brass ring herself, it seemed odd to her that he never tried to kiss her or feel her up or anything. Just as she was beginning to suspect he might be gay (it would go a long way towards explaining those tight t-shirts), he finally initiated some contact that went beyond the standard friendly hugs they always exchanged. It happened at Astro-Burger on Santa Monica Boulevard, where they were grabbing some dinner before Angie's shift at The Starbucket began. Of course, Johnny had somewhere to be and had bummed a ride from Angie. While they stood at the counter waiting to order, he'd gently — and quite casually — rested his hand on the curve of her rump. After several weeks of not a damn thing, his hand on her ass felt so startlingly weird to Angie that she leapt awkwardly away from him, banging her knee on the counter and cursing loudly. As with his endless double-entendres, he pretended the ass-touch hadn't happened, but Angie had a feeling there'd be more of that sort of thing now that the initial approach had been made.

Another week went by, during which Angie drove Johnny to several more appointments around Hollywood and the San Fernando Valley, although without any further physical contact outside of the usual hugs. For a guy with so many appointments, Johnny didn't seem to actually *do* anything that she could ascertain, and any questions about his employment or what those appointments were about wound up neatly sidestepped or laughed off. To further the annoyance, the only friends of Johnny's she'd met were Hoppy and Kurt, two fellows remarkably like Johnny in that they were outwardly charming but seemed to be nothing but surface once she gave it a little thought.

One morning — exactly eight days after the ass-touching event — Johnny called Angie, waking her up after a long shift at the bar. He needed some new headshots and wondered if she'd mind meeting up with him and taking some photos. In her semi-coherent state, she agreed, and soon found herself driving to an address in North Holly-wood. As she sat in traffic, bleary-eyed and clutching a cup of coffee between her thighs, it finally struck her: *Who the hell is this guy, and more importantly, what the hell am I doing?* The good Mr. Jerkov offered nothing in the way of real friendship but was always quick to ask for a favor, and whenever Angie found herself becoming angry about it, he simply turned on the charm and before long she was telling herself *Aw, that's just Johnny*.

Well, screw Johnny. She'd go ahead and take the pictures he needed since she'd already agreed to it, but afterwards, she'd tell him to lose her phone number and never darken her doorstep again. The guy never even kicked in any cash for the gas she used in hauling him around the city, for Christ's sake.

Angie pulled up to the curb at the address Johnny had given her, leaning across the tiny car to look out at the storefront. It was a rather shady-looking Karate school, its name scrawled in fat, faded magic marker across a large sheet of poster board, affixed to the inside of the window with yellowing cellophane tape. Some effort had been exerted in an attempt to give the lettering an Asian look, but the result was largely indecipherable — she thought the school might be called *Yum Yum Fighting Man*, but surely that couldn't be right. A ratty, busted-plastic sign reading *LOSED* rested in the bottom corner of the window. Hotel-style blackout curtains blocked the interior from view. Angie was about to drive away when Johnny poked his head out the door of the place, telling her to come on in. Today's choice of t-shirt was the tightest she'd seen yet, delineating Johnny's smallish pot belly and making his freakishly-erect nipples jut out as if pencil stubs had been wedged between the fabric and his man-teats. Instead of his usual jeans, he was clad in a pair of disquietingly short denim cutoffs and a pair of ridiculous tube socks with red stripes at their tops. The only fashion selection Johnny had made that Angie even marginally approved of were the black high-top Converse All-Stars.

As Angie entered the Karate school — a small front room with some filthy mats spread about the floor, a door marked *Sensei Steve* leading to a back room — she was hit with a strange odor, like a combination of sweaty feet and Elmer's Glue. Johnny went for the predictable hug, his nipples poking Angie and making her wince. Releasing her, he shut the front door, then turned to give her that big stupid-making grin.

It won't work this time, buddy, Angie thought.

Johnny handed her a small digital camera.

"I don't really know how to work this thing," Angie cautioned.

"It'll be fine," Johnny assured her, walking to the center of the room. Smiling, he unfastened his cutoffs and let them drop around his striped tube socks, revealing his rather substantial dangling dong.

Angie simply stood there for a very long moment.

"What the hell is this," she finally asked.

Jerkov, as it turned out, was not a Polish name, but a *pornish* one — Johnny had designs on becoming an adult film superstar, and needed some full-body shots, displaying his talent in its relaxed state as well as its furious battle-ready mode.

Angie stared on in shock as Johnny gripped his member, gazing weirdly at her as he began doing exactly what his last name sounded like. "It'll be ready in a second," he muttered. "This is okay with you, right?"

Hit it with the camera and run like hell, Angie's mind screamed, yet she found herself unable to move.

And that was when the heretofore-unknown *Mrs.* Jerkov

entered the Karate school.

"Son of a bitch," Mrs. Jerkov (a.k.a. Lucy Davis, for that was Johnny's real last name) said, oddly calm.

Johnny's eyes widened in surprise, yet he continued yanking on himself. "It's just business, Lucy," he said, working that smile.

"Are you paying him to — to fiddle with himself?" Mrs. Jerkov asked Angie, looking at her as if she'd just bought some magic beans.

"Wait now — who are you?" Angie sized up her escape route, wondering if she could slip past Mrs. Jerkov and out the door.

"I'm his wife. And if you said you'd pay him to do — *that*, you'd better follow through."

"You're okay with this?" Angie asked, not quite sure she'd heard Mrs. Jerkov correctly.

Mrs. Jerkov let out a little snort. "I'm just happy he's earning some money."

Johnny smiled again, still tugging at himself.

"Here," Angie said, handing the camera to Mrs. Jerkov and heading for the door. "Adios, Lord and Lady Jerkoff."

Banging the door shut behind her, Angie scurried to her car and coaxed it into the closest approximation of peeling out a Geo Metro will do, leaving the Jerkovs and *Yum Yum Fighting Man* behind. Johnny called her several times over the next few days, but Angie didn't answer. Eventually he gave up, no doubt moving on to the next sucker.

So yeah, after that whole experience, a little anxiety from Pete seemed pretty reasonable in Angie's book. Like she'd told Suzanne, Pete was a normal guy, and it was tough to find one of those in Los Angeles. Checking the address again, Angie guided the little car into a left turn, still feeling a little worried about how Pete would react to her surprise visit, but no longer so concerned that she was being manipulative. Johnny Jerkov, *he* was manipulative. Not being honest with Pete about her history? That was just... erring on the side of caution.

Everything's gonna be just fine, she told herself as she pulled up to the curb outside Pete's apartment building. Hell, she even got lucky with a parking space.

25

"Are you the bride of the beast?"

Angie stood at Pete's apartment door, fist poised to knock. She stared at the old man down the corridor, who seemed to be trying to *loom*, his tiny stature preventing it from happening. "Excuse me?"

Mr. Stovall calmly opened the small brown suede bag slung over his shoulder — obviously an old purse, adorned with a trio of smiley faces, also cut from thin leather — and pulled out a sharpened wooden stake, politely displaying it for Angie.

"Umm..." Puzzled, she cocked a thumb toward Pete's door.

Mr. Stovall nodded happily, pleased that Angie seemed to get it.

"I think I'm more like the dinner date of the beast," she said, trying not to appear too frantic as she knocked on the door.

"It's a bit early for dinner," Mr. Stovall pointed out.

Angie smiled at him, simultaneously knocking a bit more emphatically. After a few moments, the door opened just the tiniest bit, Pete's sleepy face visible in the shadows within. "How's what?" he mumbled.

"Hey Pete I'm here for coming inside," Angie blurted, shoving her way into Pete's apartment. Pete blinked at her, groggy, as she quickly shut the door behind her and smiled at him. "Hi. You got some weirdos in this building." Noticing the darkness of the apartment — not to mention Pete's bleary-eyed appearance — she added "Oh shit — did I wake you up?"

Pete rubbed his left eye. "No, I had to get up to answer the door." Gesturing awkwardly for her to follow, he shuffled over towards the bed. "C'mon in." As he settled his butt down on the mattress, his stomach cut loose with a rumbling, rolling squeal, like hamsters inside a salad spinner.

Angie flopped onto the bed next to him. "Sounds like I got here just in time."

Pete put a hand to his belly as if to muffle its cries. He'd planned to swing by the goat farm after his date with Angie the previous night, but instead he'd barely gotten the Duster back into storage and made it home before the sun came up. His grogginess was as much from lack of food as from his insomnia — he felt practically delirious.

"Look at your li'l pajants," Angie said, grinning.

"What?" Pete shot a mortified look towards the crotch of his red plaid pajamas, afraid something had slipped loose somehow.

"Your little flannel jammie pants, your pajants," Angie explained.

"Am I dreaming this?"

"That's the sweetest thing anyone's ever said to me."

"It is?" Befuddled, Pete screwed his knuckles into his eyes, trying to force the sleepiness away. "Is it — wait, is it daytime?"

"Yeah," Angie said, nodding toward Pete's clock radio.

He turned to look at the bright red display: 2:57. Squinting, he checked for the little dot in the corner. It was lit. "PM," he muttered.

"I got a call from my boss," Angie said. "Suzanne flaked out last night and he hasn't been able to get a hold of her, so I've gotta work her shift tonight."

"Flaked out?" Pete asked.

"Yeah, didn't even lock up the bar. But I was thinking, maybe we could just grab an early dinner before I go in?"

Pete was still parsing all this, particularly the notion that Suzanne left The Starbucket without locking up. "Is that normal?"

"Having dinner early?" Angie asked. "You really are sleepy, aren't you?"

"Yeah, but — no," Pete said. "Suzanne taking off like that, not locking up."

"I don't really know her all that well, but she seems a little flighty sometimes. I guess it wouldn't surprise me."

Something's not right. Pete gazed blankly at the floor for a moment, then looked at Angie as a thought occurred to him. "How did you find my apartment?"

"Googled it."

"Goog — the Internet?"

"Yeah," she said. "Got your address, driving directions, and a picture of the front of your building."

"Holy shit. Can *anyone* do that?"

"No. I'm actually a killer robot from the future," Angie

said. "It's the Internet, dude — anybody can find anything."

"Yipes," Pete said. That was almost certainly not a good thing.

"So about this dinner..." Angie slid closer to him, her hip bumping up against his. "I'm thinkin' Fatburger."

The touch of Angie's body against his finally snapped Pete out of it enough to realize exactly what she was suggesting. "Fat — I can't go to any Fatburger!" he exclaimed with something close to panic.

"Sure ya can," Angie said. "They let anybody in there."

Shooting to his feet, Pete walked a few steps away from the bed. "No, no, we have to wait, I can't —"

"Is it your diet? Because we could go somewhere else. You like Thai?"

Waving his hands frantically, Pete began pacing in a tight little circle. "It's not about Thai or burgers or whatever — I just can't go outside."

"Not in your pajants, you can't, " Angie teased.

"I can't go outside in pants-pants, either."

Angie's face screwed into a perplexed frown. Maybe she *had* blown it by showing up unannounced. "What are you talking about, what's wrong with you?"

Not answering, Pete continued to pace.

Angie got up, grabbing his arm playfully. "C'mon, I'll drive, and I'll even let you wear your pajants —"

"I can't go —"

"Come on —"

"—Outside!" Exasperated, Pete yanked his arm from her grasp and stepped away from Angie, staring at her. "Because *I'm a vampire.*"

As the look of confusion spread across Angie's face, Pete suddenly felt very embarrassed.

"Oh," Angie said softly, unsure of her footing. Dredging up a tiny smile, she forged ahead. "Look, I know how it is, you work nights, things get weird…"

"No," Pete said, shaking his head. "That's not it."

Angie hesitated. "Then tell me what it is."

Screwing up his courage, Pete looked her square in the eyes — those beautiful, friendly eyes, suddenly full of hurt, and hoped like hell he wasn't about to make it even worse. "I'm… a foul creature of the night, pretty much."

Angie's face slowly took on the classic New Yorker *you-gotta-be-shittin'-me* look of disbelief. "A vampire," she said, voice flat.

"Drinker of blood," Pete said.

Angie let that sink in for a few seconds, then thrust a hand out, gesturing around the room. "So where's your coffin?"

"I have a twin bed," Pete said. "I'm a vampire with a twin bed. That's just the way it is."

Eyes narrowing, Angie studied him for another long moment. "Look, I thought we had a good time last night, but if you don't wanna go out with me, just say so. Don't feed me a line."

"I *do* wanna go out with you —"

"Then what's all this vampire bullshit?"

Once again displaying an uncanny knack for inopportune timing, Pete's stomach yowled vociferously. Angie's eyes flicked to his belly, then back to his face, waiting for — *demanding* — an answer.

How the hell do I do this? Pete looked around the room.

Windows. Of course.

Returning his attention to Angie, Pete cleared his throat, then walked to the nearest window. Another glance at Angie. She was watching him intently, her gaze somehow steely and puzzled all at once.

Sighing, Pete turned to the window and began peeling away the duct tape holding the blind firmly to the wall.

"You'd better not be thinkin' you're gonna jump out that window and run," Angie said.

"I'm not going anywhere." As he pulled the tape away, a tiny sliver of sunlight hit his right hand, instantly burning the skin. "Ow," he yelped, yanking his hand back out of the light. He looked towards Angie, hoping she'd seen it happen and that might be all the proof she'd need. Nope. It figured.

Tugging the strip of tape completely away from the blind, Pete wadded it up and tossed it on the floor. Gingerly taking hold of the blind, he pulled it away from the window, allowing a narrow shaft of sunlight into the room. "Oh boy," he said softly.

Steeling himself, Pete tilted his head towards the window and into the light.

Angie's mouth fell open as Pete's scalp began to sizzle and smoke.

"Ow ow ow ow *ow!*" Pete hollered, stepping back from the shaft of light and letting the blind fall back into place. He looked at Angie, his head still smoldering. "See?"

Eyes wide, Angie took a couple hesitant steps towards Pete. As she stared at him, the burn on his head was already healing. Slowly extending her hand, she touched the remnants of the burn. She could feel the flesh repairing itself beneath her fingertips, the hair beginning to grow back.

"Ow," Pete reiterated.

Angie trailed her fingers down Pete's face and beneath his chin. "You know your neighbor wants to drive a stake through your heart, right?"

"Mr. Stovall? He's harmless."

Angie gazed at Pete as strands of hair sprouted from the pink flesh on his scalp, growing like a bean in a time-lapse grade-school science film. "Wow," she said.

"*Wow* is not the response I expected." Pete reached up to gently scratch at the new skin atop his head.

"Yeah, well, Dracula isn't the boyfriend I expected," Angie said.

"Boyfriend?"

"Did I say that out loud?"

Pete shook his head, amazed. "Man, you're taking this really well."

"I dunno, maybe I'm kind of in shock," she said, stepping back towards the bed and sitting down. "I can't guarantee I won't freak out a little in a few hours. But I believe in ghosts and Bigfoot and shit, so I guess I can live with the idea that vampires are real." She patted the mattress next to her. "Besides, you're cute as hell."

Smiling, Pete sat down next to her. "Bigfoot?"

"Don't be tellin' me Bigfoot isn't real."

He cautiously scratched the top of his head again. The wound had completely healed, the hair grown back in, albeit slightly longer and curlier than the rest of Pete's mop. "You know, if I hadn't handled that little demonstration just right, my whole head could've gone up in flames."

"Yeah?" Angie inched closer to him. "Maybe I'd better kiss it a little." Entangling her fingers in his hair, she tilted his head forward and pressed her lips to the injured spot. "Ooh, that's kinda weird," she said, flicking the tip of her tongue across her lips, as if tasting something. "It's tingly — kind of like licking a battery."

Pete's nose crinkled. "Really?"

"Yeah."

"I don't know how this stuff works," Pete said.

"C'mere." Angie leaned back on the bed, pulling Pete down on top of her. She kissed him on the lips this time, her tongue probing into his mouth. After several very long moments, she broke the kiss and cocked an eyebrow at him. "How come you don't have fangs?"

Pete's tongue slid across his canines. "They only come out when I need 'em," he said, self-conscious.

"Can you make it happen?" Angie said, eyes alight with curiosity.

"Yeah," Pete said reluctantly. "But that's kinda like running with scissors. Bad idea."

"Whatever, Suzie Safety." Angie wrapped her arms around his neck, pulling him close.

Pete was painfully aware of the shrieking and howling emanating from his stomach as he and Angie sank deeper into each other's arms, but she didn't seem to be concerned with such things.

Within a few minutes, Pete wasn't, either.

26

Little Samantha Rogers always wanted to be a vampire, or at least from the time she was seven and came home from school to find something called *Dark Shadows* on TV. Her mother and father told her vampires weren't real, that Barnabas Collins was just an actor, but Samantha knew better. At night, she'd ever-so-quietly slip from her bed, tiptoe across the room, and open her window, wishing for Barnabas to come visit her as she stood in the cool blue moonlight.

He never did.

To her parents' chagrin, Samantha raised herself on a steady diet of vampire cinema, books and television. She dressed in blacks and reds, and always — *always* — insisted on vintage clothing, leading her mother and father to speculate wildly as to where the hell their little girl even learned the *term* vintage, let alone how she decided it was going to be her style. She avoided playing outside in the daytime; her parents took to shoving her out the door and locking it behind her in hopes their daughter would finally get some sun on her pale skin. On those occasions, Samantha would scamper away from the house and find a place to hide, somewhere safe from the sun's deadly rays. On her first date — she was fifteen — she bit her young man on the neck, hard enough to draw blood. During the double-barreled four-parent scolding that followed, she claimed it was merely a hickey gone wrong. As the tale spread throughout her school, she was equally shunned as a weirdo and pursued as a tramp.

Immediately upon graduating high school, little Samantha — now a big girl — hopped a city bus to Jumbo's Clown Room on Hollywood Boulevard, where she took a job as an exotic dancer. There, she was able to work nights, and her ghost-white skin and womanly curves brought in a substantial amount of tips. Men and women alike sought her favor — and some of them didn't mind it when she'd bite. Samantha settled into a comfortable, if somewhat unusual, life.

But throughout all of this, she never stopped wishing for

that visit from Barnabas.

When she was twenty-three, a vampire finally came calling.

Probably looking for an easy meal on a boring evening, Carson Fitzgerald had strolled into Jumbo's, taking a seat near the back, in the shadows. Somehow, Samantha knew what he was the instant she saw him — the confident way he carried himself, the air of seductive menace that enfolded him like a cloak. And the eyes... those dark, lethal eyes.

Unwilling to give him a chance to choose one of the other girls, Samantha went to Fitzgerald and struck up a conversation. When her shift ended, they left together.

That night, Carmella Crimsonella was born.

She knew it sounded a bit silly, but it was the vampire name she'd chosen for herself as a little girl; it seemed regal to her then, and she'd flirted with using it as her stage name at Jumbo's, but it was too special. It was her *vampire name*.

Carmella continued working at Jumbo's for several months after that, until she realized there was easier money to be had by choosing her victims for their wealth — and their fetishes. Most of the men and women she fed upon were happy to provide her with compensation for her unique services. Those who didn't opt to pay met with untimely ends, and Carmella helped herself to whatever cash and interesting belongings they left behind. Within a few years, she opened Club Emoglobin, providing not only a friendly environment for the other vampires in Hollywood, but a constant supply of fresh food.

Of all the vampires at the Club, Carmella was the only one who slept in a coffin. She had a bed, of course — one needed a comfortable arena for certain events — but even on nights when she brought someone in to share that bed,

Carmella always retired to the coffin, alone. It was the way Barnabas slept, in the basement of the old Collins house, and it made her feel safe.

Tonight, though, Carmella lay awake, staring at the closed coffin lid above her and wondering if this would be the night the vampire came back for her.

Francois le Sanguine had called her shortly after sunset (she kept her cell phone handy, even in the coffin — modern times, after all), weeping and wailing as he delivered the news that Bertrand was dead, his head severed, his blood drained. Fitzgerald had sacrificed one of his children to send a message to the others.

Nearly an hour had passed since the call. Carmella was afraid to move, terrified that she'd push open the lid of her coffin to find Fitzgerald smiling down at her, dagger in his hand. She tried to remember the last time she'd been scared of anything, let alone a vampire. *The monkey.* That was it, the only thing that had ever scared her. The toy belonged to her father — one of those battery-operated monkeys that violently bashed a pair of cymbals together. Smack it on the head and it would stop, bulge its eyes, bare its teeth and shriek horribly. Little Samantha was petrified by it, afraid she'd find it in her bed some night, eyes bulging at her as it screeched and clanged.

She reached up, slowly lifting the coffin lid — just a crack, just enough to peek out. Eyes wide, holding her breath, Carmella peered through the narrow opening. Nothing. *But he could simply be standing on the other side of the coffin...*

Her phone rang. Jerking wildly, Carmella cracked her head against the lid of the coffin. Swearing, she shoved the lid all the way open, sitting up to look around the room —

Again, nothing. She was alone.

Relaxing, she checked the phone. Elric Dreadsbane. He was probably downstairs in the Club, wondering why she wasn't at work yet. She let it go to voicemail.

Carmella had forced a promise from Francois; that he'd leave it to her to tell the others about Bertrand. The last thing she needed was one high-strung, prissy vampire telling another that one of their own had been killed — it'd be like a bunch of frightened Chihuahuas quivering and yipping at each other. Pinball, she'd handle the news okay, but Elric was going to go off like an anguish-bomb, expelling sorrow-shrapnel across a city block. A few months earlier during disco night at the Club, Elric had burst into tears when the DJ played *Shadow Dancing*, blubbering and sobbing that he'd never gotten over the death of Andy Gibb. Carmella felt reasonably certain he wasn't going to take Bertrand's murder any better.

It occurred to Carmella that Bertrand's death meant not a thing to her, except to trigger the fear that she might be next. She'd known him for years, and they were close — a little *too* close on occasion, probably — but to be honest, she'd suffered more grief when Andy Gibb died, herself. And she was no disco fan.

She looked around the small room where her coffin lay atop its pedestal. With her childhood hero's resting place in mind, she'd hired a Hollywood set designer to turn the room into a proper Gothic chamber, with faux stone walls and floor, ancient-looking wooden beams overhead. Heavy velvet drapes adorned the shuttered windows. Iron candelabra jutted from the walls, tendrils of wax spilling over them. It had been home for many years, her safe haven. Now it just seemed hollow and false, nothing more than the movie set it was.

Carmella preferred to sleep in the nude, but her lack of clothing suddenly made her feel helpless and exposed. One arm held across her breasts, she clambered from the coffin and padded across the floor to her wardrobe, where she began getting dressed. Briefly, she considered the notion of closing the Club for the night, or possibly even the week, then thought better of it. Smarter, she thought, to surround herself with as many people as possible — Fitzgerald surely wouldn't launch an all-out frontal assault on a nightclub full of witnesses, would he?

As much as she hated to admit it, Carmella was beginning to think Pete Tyler was the only one of the bunch who had any goddamn sense; getting out of town seemed like a very good idea indeed.

27

Pete could never remember which particular act represented which base, but he was reasonably sure he'd rounded third and gone all the way home, even if it was on a ground ball and not a spectacular out-of-the-park homer. And considering his lack of practice over the last few — *Jesus!* — decades, he'd only stumbled one time that he knew of, and that was early on, just after Angie had wriggled out of her jeans and panties.

"Wow," Pete said, feeling around. "It's all, uh, Kojak down here."

"Kojak?" Angie lifted her head to look at him. "How

long has it been since you made out with a girl?"

"Uh, last night, thanks," Pete said.

She jabbed him with an elbow, causing him to grunt sharply. "Before that."

"1973. And that was just kissing."

"Good God," Angie said. "So you're used to that crazy hippie-style bush."

Pete's eyebrows went up a little, his cheeks going red. "Well, I'm not sure how *used* to it I was — it's not like I was Jim Morrison or something." He gently felt between Angie's legs again. "But I do remember these things being…" He hesitated, his ability to concentrate going slightly haywire as his fingers did the walking.

"What?"

"Fuzzy," Pete said, snapping out of it. "You know, fluffy."

"Are you complaining?"

"Not in the least," Pete asserted.

After that, things went remarkably well. There were no more significant and/or unexpected changes in the female anatomy that caught Pete off guard, and to be honest, he quite enjoyed the Kojak-style grooming of Angie's nether regions. His bed squeaked like it had a nest of rats in it and at one point he kicked his lava lamp off the bedside table, but overall, it was a solid comeback — and most important-ly, Angie seemed quite pleased by the whole thing.

When the dust settled, they lay on their backs, crammed tightly together on the narrow twin-bed mattress, the fallen lava lamp casting an eerie reddish glow from where it had rolled under the bed. Pete worried that his plentiful body hair brushing against Angie's smooth skin might freak her out, but she didn't try to squirm away from him, and he took that as a good sign.

"What time do you have to be at work?" he asked.

"I don't know — now? Soon? What time is it?"

Pete flopped his head to the side, checking the clock. "It's a little after seven-thirty."

"Very very soon, then," Angie said, not making any move to get up.

A freakish wail emanated from Pete's stomach once again. He winced as Angie looked at him.

"Uh-oh," she said. "My head's not startin' to look like a big juicy steak, is it?"

Embarrassed, Pete sat up, hand resting on his belly. "No."

Angie sat up next to him, resting her chin on his shoulder. "I, uh... I know it's gotta be a weird subject for you, but whatta you... I mean, who do you..." she trailed off, unsure of how to put it.

"Whose blood do I drink, is that what you're asking?" Pete said.

"Yeah."

Pete turned his head so his nose was touching hers and nuzzled her just a bit. "Goats," he muttered, very quietly.

Angie thought about that for a moment. "In Los Angeles?"

"There's a bunch of ranches outside of L.A., in the valley," Pete explained. "I go out there and — you know... I drink the... blood... of goats." He cocked his head back to check her expression, see if she looked like she might be about to run or call the cops or something. "But I never kill 'em, I just drink a little. That's why I'm hungry all the time." His brow furrowed as something occurred to him. "Now that I think about it, I hope I haven't been creating a legion of vampire goats." His belly squealed again, as if excited by the loose talk of goats and feeding.

Angie put her hand over Pete's, feeling his belly rumble with hunger. "You never drink human blood?"

Pete fixed her with a sincere gaze. "I don't wanna be a vampire, Angie."

She sat there for a few moments, head still resting on Pete's shoulder, casually trailing her thumb through the hair on his belly. It tickled like hell, and just when he thought he couldn't take any more, she lifted her head to look around the room. "Where'd my pants end up? I gotta get to the bar."

Pete glanced around, spotting the wad of jeans lying on the floor across the room, panties still tangled in the legs. "I got 'em," he said, getting to his feet. He was painfully aware of his nudity as he shuffled over to Angie's pants, and painstakingly tried to avoid shooting her a moon as he bent to retrieve them. She slid to the edge of the bed as he brought them to her, the lava lamp doing an interesting job of illuminating her naked breasts.

"Is there anything you miss?" she asked, taking the jeans from Pete and slipping her feet into them. "You know, about being… not a vampire." She stood, tugging her jeans up over her hips and fastening them.

"Food," Pete said, opening a drawer and grabbing a pair of his own jeans.

"I figured that much," Angie said. As Pete wrestled his way into his pants, she nosed around the floor near the bed. "Shirt?"

Pete scanned the area. "Under the bed?"

Angie ducked down to peer beneath the bed. "Nope. Got one I can borrow?"

The question sent a little thrill running up Pete's spine.

That's totally a girlfriend thing to do, wearing a guy's shirt, he thought. Trying not to appear overly excited, he went to his closet and started flipping through the options.

"So you can't eat normal food at all?" Angie asked, watching him.

"Nope, makes me sick." He settled on a Black Sabbath 1978 tour shirt, holding it out for her approval.

"That'll work." Handing her the shirt, Pete watched as she slipped into it. As her head poked through the collar, she had a tiny grin on her face. "Okay?"

"Heck yeah," Pete said, admiringly. He turned back to the closet, grabbing a white undershirt and one of his denim work shirts.

"Anything else?" Angie collected her shoes and sat on the bed again to put them on.

"Shirt-wise?" Pete asked, confused. He tugged the undershirt over his head.

"Anything else you miss," she said.

"Plenty." Pete pulled the work shirt on and started buttoning it. "But — this sounds goofy, probably, but one thing that really eats at me... I never got to drive the Duster in the daytime," he said, wistful.

Angie finished tying her shoes and looked up at him. "Really?"

"Yeah. I bought it after dark, when I got off work. Then later that night, I got... you know, *bit*." He looked at Angie. "Bitten?"

"That's a damn shame, is what that is."

Pete nodded. "Man, I'd love to take that car down the PCH with the windows open and the radio blaring and the sun reflecting off the ocean —"

The apartment door blew inward off its hinges, hurtling

across the room to slam into the opposite wall.

Shocked as he was, Pete's brain still registered embarrassment that his feet actually came off the floor in surprise, then Angie's fingers balled up in the back of his shirt, nearly pulling him off balance.

Suzanne stepped into the apartment. She was still clad in her work clothes — skintight jeans and black tank top — but her skin was the color of a fish's belly after it's been left on the dock for a few hours. Her soulless eyes glared from deep in their sockets, her features sunken. Growling softly, like a beast that's just cornered its prey, she bared her fangs, a string of spittle running from the corner of her mouth.

"Suzanne —?" Angie muttered, still clinging to the tail of Pete's work shirt.

Snarling, Suzanne lunged at Angie. Pete ducked forward, driving a shoulder into the vampire and knocking her back onto his desk. He saw the Plymouth Duster model kit shatter beneath her, a tiny tire rolling across the desk.

Fingernails scrabbling at the desktop, Suzanne launched herself at Pete with insane speed, catching his hair in both hands and whirling him around. Tufts of his hair came out in her grip and he stumbled backwards into the closet, collapsing into the mess. Hissing, Suzanne was instantly on Angie, dragging her off the bed and down onto the floor.

On his back in the clutter of the closet, Pete kicked his legs and twisted, grabbing the edge of the wall to yank himself from the jumble of clothing and junk. Suzanne was on top of Angie, fangs inches above her throat, saliva dripping onto Angie's flesh as she kicked and fought and swore.

Pete scrambled across the floor, jamming an arm beneath the bed. Coming up with the lava lamp in his hand, he smashed the heavy glass into Suzanne's head. Howling, the vampire spun around, driving an elbow into Pete's groin. Tiny fireworks flared up in his vision and he flopped back onto his ass, looking up to see Mr. Stovall standing just inside the room, an odd leather bag slung over his shoulder.

"*I knew it!*" the old man hollered, awkwardly tugging a wooden stake and a mallet from the bag.

Eyes going freakishly wide upon sight of the stake, Suzanne flung herself at Mr. Stovall. Pete hit her in mid-leap, both of them coming down hard on the wrecked door and cracking it down the middle. Suzanne clawed at Pete, digging furrows down his arms. Teeth clenched against the pain, he finally managed to catch her wrists and pin her arms to the floor.

"Get her, Mr. Stovall!" he yelled.

Suddenly, the old man didn't look so sure about all this.

"The stake! Use the stake!"

Mr. Stovall just stood there, trembling slightly as Suzanne yowled and kicked and wailed, desperately trying to wriggle free from Pete's grip.

"Come ON!" Pete shouted.

Darting across the room, Angie grabbed the stake from the old man's hand and dropped to her knees next to Pete. Suzanne was making sounds like a cat in a bathtub and snapping her fangs at Pete and Angie. Hesitantly, Angie positioned the stake over Suzanne's chest, shooting a glance at Mr. Stovall.

"Now, Mr. Stovall — hit it!"

The old man quickly shuffled forward, raised the mallet, then froze, the hammer poised above the stake.

"She isn't gettin' any less vampirey!" Pete prodded.

"I can't do it," Mr. Stovall whimpered.

Angie snatched the mallet from Mr. Stovall. As Suzanne continued to hiss and fight, Angie and Pete exchanged a look, then, taking a deep breath, Angie brought the mallet down, bashing the stake a couple inches into Suzanne's chest. Eyes bulging, Suzanne released an unearthly wail. Grunting, Angie hammered the stake deeper, then deeper still. With one last bellowing scream, Suzanne's cries ended and her thrashing and twisting ceased. A second later, her body exploded into fine ash, filling the apartment with a cloud of gray dust.

"Holy shit," Angie said, choking.

"We've gotta get out of here," Pete said.

"Holy *shit*, do you realize what we just did?"

"Angie, we've gotta go. Now." Pete got to his feet, pulling Angie up.

"What about her —"

"Forget it," Pete said, remembering to grab his boots. "Go back to your apartment and lock the door," he told Mr. Stovall.

The old man watched as Pete led Angie out of the ravaged apartment and down the hall. After a few moments, he looked down at the wooden stake resting amidst the ash of Suzanne's body. "Apartment full of *vampires*," he said very softly.

28

Pete's work truck sped along the 210 freeway, heading east on their way out of Los Angeles. Pete didn't know exactly where they were headed, he only knew they had to get the hell out of L.A.

He glanced over at Angie, her head resting against the passenger window as if she didn't have the strength to hold it up. She'd been completely silent ever since he dragged her out of the apartment — not surprising, considering everything she'd been subjected to over the last few hours. Well, minus the good part, he hoped.

Pete shifted in his seat, wincing at the pain in his crotch where Suzanne had nailed him. Fortunately, she'd missed his balls with the bony end of her elbow, but she'd caught him just at the top of the inner thigh, and — ask anyone — that will light a fella up pretty good, too.

"I wasn't honest with you last night," Angie said, the sound of her voice startling Pete after the long period of silence.

"What?" Pete asked. "About what?"

She turned to look at him, her expression almost frighteningly empty. "About why I left Brooklyn. It wasn't a — a bad boyfriend situation or anything."

"You don't have to talk about it if you don't want to," Pete said.

"I want to," Angie insisted. "I think I owe it to you." She twisted, folding her left leg up in the seat so she was facing Pete. "I left because of my dad — well, because of my dad's... nocturnal activities."

"Oh shit," Pete said. "Your dad's a vampire."

"What?" Angie said, surprised. "No, my dad's not a vampire, if my dad was a vampire I wouldn't have been surprised to find out I'm *dating* a vampire or that my friend — or whatever Suzanne was — got turned into one, I'd be like, goddammit, not more friggin' vampires."

Ohhh I don't think I like where this is going, Pete thought, expecting the worst.

"My dad," Angie began, pausing to suck in a deep breath, "Is a second-story man."

Pete looked at her for a second, then laughed. "He's a what?"

Angie frowned, a little irked by Pete's reaction. "A second-story man, a criminal."

"I know what a second-story man is," Pete said. "I'm just, I'm surprised — I mean, you thought your dad being a burglar was gonna scare me off?"

"Well, up until you set your head on fire with nothing but sunlight, it seemed like something to be concerned about, yes," Angie said.

"Why did that make you leave New York?"

"He got into some serious trouble with some serious troublemakers. Started tryin' to drag me into the whole thing, and I didn't want any part of it. Figured I'd be better off on the other side of the country."

"And now you've got vampire trouble," Pete said.

Angie slid towards him, resting a hand on his thigh. "I can't believe I killed Suzanne."

"I know it probably doesn't help, but she was already dead."

"Then what are *you*? Are *you* dead?" Angie asked, that initial shock she'd mentioned earlier finally beginning to give way to a potential wig-out. "Because that kinda freaks me out."

Pete wrestled for the words, hoping to ease Angie's mind a bit. "Okay, technically I guess *undead* is the better way to put it... if that helps... at all."

Angie thought that one over for a moment. "But I don't

understand — why Suzanne? How did it even happen?"

"It's a long story," Pete said. "But the vampire who turned me — Carson Fitzgerald — it was his way of sending me a message." He looked at Angie. "I'm so sorry. I never should've gotten close to you, it was stupid."

"Don't say that." Her grip tightened on his leg.

Something outside the truck was roaring. No, *flapping*. Movement caught his eye and Pete looked back at the road just as a shape — massive, black and very, very fast — whipped past the windshield. Whatever it was hit the top of the truck like a linebacker, rocking the vehicle. Pete fought the wheel as four-inch claws tore through the metal of the truck's roof, peeling it back.

Angie recoiled against the passenger door as the roof was torn open like a cardboard box being pulled apart. She didn't get a good look at what was up there, but it had big goddamn teeth. Unable to hold it back any longer, she screamed.

The truck careened back and forth across the highway as Pete struggled to keep it under control. Suddenly the thing's hideous clawed hand thrust into the cab, grasping at Angie. As she cowered in terror, Pete took one hand off the steering wheel, grabbing for her —

Too late.

Pete watched in horror as Angie was yanked through the hole where the roof used to be, disappearing into the night sky.

The truck went sideways into a four-wheel slide, skidding off the road and spinning out in the dirt, kicking up a huge cloud of dust and coming to a stop some distance from the highway. Pete's door banged open and he was out, running, screaming Angie's name to the sky.

A rush of wind and something hit him, hard. Pete went airborne, his legs clipping the top of the truck's work bed and flipping him end over end as he went over the other side. He slammed painfully to the ground, the wind going out of him. Lifting his head, he squinted through the dust and the pain, looking beneath the truck to where a pair of male feet stood on the other side.

"Fitzgerald…" Pete wheezed.

Reaching up, Pete grabbed the truck's rear bumper and dragged himself to his feet. As he straightened, he found himself looking into Fitzgerald's sneering face, fangs bared, Angie's unconscious form draped over his shoulder.

"You have much to do and very little time," Fitzgerald hissed.

Pete only saw a flash of movement, but he sure as hell felt the back of the truck come out of nowhere to hit him in the face. Then the lights went out.

* * *

Pete's left eye fluttered open, but the right didn't seem to be working. Slowly, he realized that side of his face was pressed into the dirt. With agonizing effort, he lifted his head to look around. The truck was at the bottom of a slight embankment, out of sight of the highway. For all intents and purposes, he seemed to be pretty well in the middle of nowhere.

He had a reasonably good idea how long he'd been out, thanks to the reddish glow on the horizon.

The sun was coming up.

It looked a lot like the light from his lava lamp after it rolled under his bed, Pete noticed.

29

The late afternoon sun seemed swollen with rage, relentlessly determined to get in the last few punches before it began to sink in the west. At the top of the embankment, traffic rolled past on the nearby highway, Pete's work truck hidden from view below.

Heat ripples shimmered from the twisted metal of the truck's roof and the top of the workbed, even as the sun dipped lower on the horizon. A dark, reddish-brown smear of blood adorned the back end of the vehicle where Pete's face had been introduced to the paint during Fitzgerald's attack. The extension ladder had come loose from its bindings at one end and lay cocked at an odd angle against the truck.

A trail of large, clawed footprints led towards the truck, becoming smaller and eventually human as they neared the vehicle. There was no similar trail leading away, but the dirt at the back of the truck appeared to have been kicked up and spread around by a powerful gust of wind.

Agonizingly slow, the sun began to disappear, reddening and looking more enraged as it lost its grip on the day. Finally, the last sliver of sunlight faded from the sky.

The truck rocked slightly.

Metal creaked.

One of the big toolboxes built into the workbed slowly opened.

Cautiously, Pete poked his head out from the toolbox, taking stock of the situation. After a moment, he painfully unfolded himself from the box, dropping to the ground in a cloud of dust. He lay there for several seconds, staring into the dirt. Hunger corkscrewed through his guts, so bad it was almost blinding. With a groan, he pushed himself to his feet and moved to the cab, climbing in behind the steering wheel.

Pete stared up through the shredded roof at the night sky as he turned the key, starting the engine. His eyes focused on something caught on a jagged piece of torn metal.

A few strands of long blonde hair, fluttering in the gentle evening breeze.

Pete threw it in gear and jammed his foot down on the gas pedal. The truck whipped through a 180, slinging the extension ladder away. The vehicle lurched up the embankment, almost going airborne as Pete guided it onto the highway, heading back towards Los Angeles.

30

Elric Dreadsbane nervously inched the lobby door open and peeked out into the courtyard of his apartment building. Not entirely convinced that Carson Fitzgerald wasn't lurking in the shadows, Elric darted out the door and scuttled rapidly across the courtyard, wispy white hair trailing out behind his gaunt head like the tail of a comet, purple velvet pants making a soft *whiffing* sound from the friction of his skinny upper thighs. He paused at the iron gate, anxiously nibbling at his lower lip, then pushed the gate open and hustled down the sidewalk, *whiff-whiff-whiff*ing all the way to the blue and white Mini Cooper parked half a block away, wide eyes flicking about crazily. In the darkness, his frilled black shirt, sleeves rolled up to reveal ghostly forearms, almost made it seem as if his head and hands were floating along the street. Certain he could feel Fitzgerald looming over him as he fumbled with the door handle, Elric practically leapt into the driver's seat, slamming the door and locking it.

Gripping the steering wheel tightly, he released the breath he'd been holding and settled back into his seat. For the life of him, he couldn't understand why Carmella wouldn't close the damn Club for a while. It wasn't like she needed the money, and for that matter, neither did Elric. Of course, the alternative meant sitting around his apartment by himself, shuddering and shivering at every sound, waiting for Fitzgerald to come crashing through a window like he did at Bertrand's place.

Suddenly gasping in fright, Elric spun around to check the car's back seat, half expecting Fitzgerald to lunge for him. Nothing there. Dropping his narrow butt back into the leather seat, Elric started the car and drove off, finally able to relax a little. He didn't give a damn how terrifying Fitzgerald might be, he wouldn't attack Elric in the midst of Hollywood traffic.

Unlike the other vampires at Club Emoglobin who only adopted their undead monikers after being bitten, Elric was known by that name long before he became a vampire — all the way back to sixth grade, in fact. His mom and dad tended to call the mild-mannered, freakishly pale youngster "Cameron," but to his D&D buddies, he was Elric Dreadsbane, warrior-cleric of ancient Ja'Rmon, the magical city atop Mount Grumblemoor. Little Cameron — frail and thin — was not, in fact, an albino, but his love for Michael Moorcock's famous hero inspired him to take a shot at being as eerily pale as he possibly could — this to accompany his profound melancholy, of course. He dressed in a long-sleeved hooded sweatshirt even in the hottest weather and never went outdoors without slathering himself with sunscreen, even at night. Once, in a moment of pique, the pinkish hue of his skin and the jet-black mop of hair atop his noggin led to an unfortunate incident with a bottle of household bleach, but the burns weren't too severe and the lad quickly recovered.

Cameron's flimsy and ashen frame incited a relentless onslaught of teasing at school, however, and things only got worse when a popular girl named Debbie Burgular (*"Like a burglar but not tee hee!"*) overheard one of Cameron's friends refer to him as "Elric." From that moment forth, Cameron's melancholy only grew more profound, and his awesomely cool D&D name haunted him throughout the remainder of his scholastic career.

He also — entirely of his own doing — managed to become a spectacularly whiny little candyass, inadvertently developing a handful of pathetic catchphrases as he mewled through life, including *God, Why Is It Always Me?*, the envy-tinged *How Come Nothing Good Ever Happens To Me?*, and the oft-heard *This Sucks, I'll Never Get Laid* (granted, that last one is a standard for pretty much any teenage boy, but Cameron managed to deliver it with such sniveling flair that it was elevated to a sort of performance art).

Midway through Cameron/Elric's final year of high school, his father was transferred to Los Angeles by his employer. Disinclined to suffer the nightmare of starting over at a new school with only a few months left before graduation, Elric opted for his GED and a part-time job at a gaming store. His skill at painting miniatures quickly made him a superstar in the gaming-nerd community, and soon he was supplementing his income by hiring out his thin, deft paintbrush hand to other gamers. Although his rampant self-pity remained firmly in place, he began to feel some sense of belonging.

Late one night, after a marathon — and quite boisterous — D&D campaign that raged over a period of three days, Elric left the dungeon master's Studio City home, triumphant but bloated with chips, pizza, and Chex Mix. Bone-weary, he shuffled down the darkened side street towards his parked car, the summer air damp and heavy, like a mystic cloak had been thrown around him. Approaching the 1978 Pacer his dad had given him — seven years old, ran great, but for a sun-hater like Elric, it was akin to driving around in a mobile greenhouse — he unlocked the door. As he lifted the handle, something very large came crashing through the branches of a tree several yards away, landing in a heap on the sidewalk near the car. Twigs and leaves showered the area as Elric found himself staring down at a well-dressed man who would've been surprisingly hand-some if he weren't snarling and thrashing in agony. A wooden stake protruded from the left side of his chest, rammed in deep, just beneath the clavicle. Upon sight of Elric, Carson Fitzgerald howled furiously, fangs bared, spittle dripping down his chin.

Elric responded by dampening his skintight black jeans with a single squirt of urine.

His first thought after peeing himself was to flee, run like hell back to the dungeon master's house, but something about Fitzgerald's gaze held him transfixed. Instead of hoofing it out of there, Elric calmly walked over to where the growling vampire lay writhing in the grass. The lights came on in the house, an old man peering out from behind heavy curtains to see what was going on in his front yard. Ignoring the man's muffled threats to call the police, Elric knelt alongside Fitzgerald, staring into the vampire's red-rimmed eyes. Carefully, Elric took hold of the stake with one hand, placing the palm of the other against Fitzgerald's chest. With a sharp tug, he yanked the stake free, a ribbon of blood spurting in its wake.

"NO!"

Elric spun towards the voice, bloody stake still gripped tightly in his hand. Running at him was a shirtless, wiry man, mid-40s, with close-cropped red hair and matching goatee, his eyes magnified crazily by thick eyeglasses. The vertical black-and-white stripes of his pants created a bizarre pattern as his thin legs pumped frantically. His right hand was clenched around the handle of a small sledge hammer. In his left, he carried a backpack, the sharpened points of several more stakes jutting from within.

Leaves whipped into the air as something blew past Elric. Fitzgerald slammed into the shirtless man, smashing him back into a parked car, the fender crumpling under the impact. The sledge hammer clattered away across the blacktop. The shirtless man dropped to his knees, stunned, gasping. Fitzgerald — no longer showing any ill effects of having a stake driven into his chest — casually approached the man. Smiling, Fitzgerald lifted a foot to the shirtless man's shoulder and gently pushed him back against the car. The vampire glanced over his shoulder as if making sure Elric was watching, then reached out to clutch the man's exposed throat. Still staring at Elric, Fitzgerald's fingers plunged into the flesh. The shirtless man shrieked horribly as Fitzgerald tore a bloody chunk of meat from his throat, the screams rising in pitch, then fading away to a choking gurgle. Fitzgerald stepped back, allowing the man to fall forward onto his face with a sickening, wet slap.

Foolishly, Elric looked back to see if the old man was still peering out the window, as if he'd somehow be of any help, but the old fellow had disappeared along with the light. When Elric turned back again, Fitzgerald was nearly upon him. Finally dropping the stake, Elric stared up at the vampire in sheer terror. Fitzgerald stood inches away, contemplating the frail, ghostly figure at his feet. Then he extended a hand, palm upturned.

Trembling, Elric reached up to accept the hand.

Soon afterwards, as he sat gasping for breath that he no longer needed, the shock of being reborn giving way to the newfound vitality coursing through his system, Elric noticed his lank hair falling past his face. It had gone milk-white, finally matching that of his childhood hero.

Lost in thought, Elric wheeled the Mini Cooper onto a side street and turned into the alley behind Club Emoglobin, pulling into his usual parking space. Shutting off the engine, he sat there for a bit, staring out into the night, wondering if Fitzgerald was waiting for him to step out of the car.

"I *saved* you," Elric muttered softly.

He pushed the car door open and stepped out, standing there with his eyes closed, waiting for the attack. After a few moments, Elric opened his eyes. The alley was empty.

And a brilliant idea had come to him. A way to save them all.

Pleased with himself, Elric shut the car door and walked off towards the Club, pushing the lock button on his key-chain as he went. A soft *chirp-chirp* emanated from the car, a reassuring accompaniment to the *whiff-whiff*ing of his velvet pants.

31

With the sun long gone, most of the animals had been rounded up at the small petting zoo set up in Moorpark Park in Studio City. Still loose in its pen, however, was a tiny black-and-white pygmy goat, contentedly nibbling on the shirttail of the little boy patting its head. The young fellow's parents stood nearby, Mom trying to lure the child away from the goat so they could go have dinner, while Dad's attention had been caught by the frantic-looking man running across the park towards them.

"This goat is named Walter," the little boy announced to his mom.

"I think Walter needs to go to bed, Derek." Mom smiled at the petting zoo attendant, a bored twenty-something whose expression said he had better places to be.

"I'm gonna ride Walter to school," Derek said.

The frantic-looking man rushed past Dad, nearly knocking him over.

"Hey," Dad blurted.

"Sorry," Pete said, not slowing down. He vaulted the low fence into the goat pen, snatching Walter from beneath the little boy's hand. "Sorry," Pete repeated, still on the move.

Derek, Mom, Dad and the bored attendant all watched in silence as Pete leapt the fence again on the opposite side of the pen, Walter the goat cradled in his arms. In an attempt to throw off any would-be pursuers, Pete ran north for several yards, looked back over his shoulder, then zigged east, back in the direction he'd come from.

"Hey," Dad ineffectually hollered after him.

Ohmigod ohmigod I'm gonna get caught, Pete fretted, his feet pounding the grass as he ran. Hunger gnawed at his guts, his stomach twisting and flipping. There was no time to drive out to his usual feeding grounds, but somehow he'd tracked this little goat by scent, using some kind of creepy vampire ability that — to be quite honest — he wasn't real happy to learn he had. Upon sight of the tiny beast, Pete's fangs had burst forth, drool running over his lower lip and down his chin. Now he fought to keep from sinking them into the goat as he ran for his truck. Didn't wanna horrify little Derek any more than he already had, after all.

Reaching the edge of the park, Pete dodged a car in the street, banged off the side of his mangled truck, and, balancing the goat in one arm, managed to pull the door open. He pushed Walter over to the passenger side and jumped in, throwing an embarrassed wave to the folks at the petting zoo as he fled the scene of the crime.

32

Mrs. Richard Weil, 71, was a good citizen. She watered her lawn in the evening — after dark — because that's what good citizens do. She recycled, even her used aluminum foil. On walks, if her terrier Matlock made a poop, she picked it up in a plastic bag. And she made a point of telling all those things to the police after the incident.

Mrs. Weil had been watering — after dark — the front lawn of her house on Radford Avenue, not far from

Moorpark Park, when Matlock began barking at something. This was not an unusual occurrence; Matlock was prone to raising the alarm at the slightest provocation, but when Mrs. Weil followed her dog's gaze and saw the beat-up white truck parked a couple houses down, swaying awkwardly from side to side, its roof practically torn off, she knew Matlock was onto something.

When she heard what sounded like a goat bleating plaintively, Mrs. Weil became well and truly concerned.

Stunned, Mrs. Weil watched the truck for several moments as the swaying continued, the bleating grew in volume, Matlock's barking became more feverish, and the water from her hose began to run out over the sidewalk and into the street. It was this last thing that finally snapped her out of it — wasting water was not the mark of a good citizen.

As she directed the spray of water back onto her lawn, she heard a *thunk* as the passenger door of the truck was shoved open. It was difficult to tell, the light being what it was, but looking towards what was no doubt a scene of terrible perversity, she saw what appeared to be a rather wholesome-looking fellow gently lower a small goat to the sidewalk.

"Sorry, little fella," the wholesome-looking fellow said to the goat as it wobbled a few steps away, obviously dazed.

Mrs. Weil gasped. Hearing the sound, the man looked towards her, his face clouded with embarrassment — and, Mrs. Weil was sure, a smear of blood.

"That… might have looked like something it wasn't," he said. "But it wasn't, I swear."

When speaking to the police afterwards, Mrs. Weil didn't mention the fangs she thought she saw when the man smiled at her. Surely just a trick of the light, and she didn't want anyone thinking she was a crazy old lady.

"Can you see this little guy gets back to the petting zoo in Moorpark Park?" With that, the wholesome-looking fellow closed the door, started the engine, and drove off.

From her vantage point — and in the darkness — Mrs. Weil couldn't clearly see the truck's license plate, perhaps the only reason the Moorpark Park Goat Snatcher was never apprehended.

For his part, Little Walter received a police escort back to the petting zoo, where he slept soundly through the night.

33

Frantic and shaking, Pete parked the truck in the darkest spot he could find in the alley behind Club Emoglobin, just in front of Carmella Crimsonella's big black 1973 S&S Cadillac Victoria hearse. The drive over the hill and into Hollywood after his goat-snack had been the most terrifying twenty or so minutes of his life (outside of anything involving Carson Fitzgerald, that is). Constantly looking over his shoulder for the cops, worrying that the shredded roof of his truck would attract unwanted attention — not to mention his concern that the old woman who'd spotted him would just leave the goat out on the sidewalk instead of taking the poor little guy home. How the hell the other vampires could feed on humans was beyond Pete's ability to comprehend — there was just too much stuff to worry about.

His first thought had been to go straight to Fitzgerald,

but there's no way that could've ended other than badly. Pete needed food, needed to regain some of the strength he'd lost while baking in the truck's toolbox all day, sleeping fitfully between bouts of contemplating the various horrible things Fitzgerald could be doing to Angie. And he also needed a plan, which he felt he'd sort of hashed out during the drive back to L.A. As plans go, it was a pretty lousy one, but it was all he had.

Pete shoved the door open and stepped out of the truck, then took off running down the alley. At the end of the building, he stopped, collecting himself. If he was going to have any chance at all of saving Angie, he needed to get his shit together and fast. Waltzing into the Club looking freaked out and half-nuts wasn't gonna do much to persuade the others to join his cause. It was time to Kirk up.

Pete took a deep breath and started moving again. Hoping he looked a lot more Shatnerized than he felt, he rounded the building and headed for the Club's front door. The standard queue of eyelinered Goth-types was in place, Pinball checking IDs. Glancing up from her task, she spotted Pete, her eyes narrowing, lip curling in displeasure — in other words, the normal greeting Pete got from her.

"Hey, thanks for blowing me off the other night, ass-wipe," Pinball snapped.

Pete did his best to play it cool. "Somethin' came up, sorry." He walked up to Pinball and nodded towards the door. "The others inside? We need to talk."

"No shit," Pinball said. She pushed the door open and led Pete inside.

The dance floor squirmed and writhed to the shitty techno beat pounding from the massive sound system. No matter how many times Pete heard the stuff, he always had a tough time reconciling the use of the word *music* in describing it. As he and Pinball waded through the crowd, Pete's dirty jeans and old t-shirt garnered disapproving sneers from the black-and-flouncy-shirts gang.

Pinball took Pete down the back hallway, past its mysterious rooms to the door at the far end. He stared at Pinball's knuckles as they rapped against the door, wondering how many teeth they'd separated from their owners. Realizing he was shifting his weight from foot to foot like a little kid who needed to pee, Pete forced himself to stand still, nervously glancing at Pinball. "Was that some kinda secret knock?"

Pinball stared at him like he was the stupidest thing she'd ever encountered.

After a moment, Carmella's muffled voice came through the door. "You alone?"

"No," Pinball said. "The idiot's with me."

"Pete?" Carmella asked.

Pete frowned. "She assumes the idiot is me?"

"Yup," Pinball said, as Carmella unlocked the door and cautiously opened it.

Pete followed Pinball into the back room, with its goofy haunted-castle decor. Elric Dreadsbane was draped across a couch, while Francois le Whatever stood nearby, puffing on a clove cigarette. Pete wanted to punch everyone in the room right in their prissy faces. Didn't they have a goddamn clue what they were dealing with? He turned to face Carmella as she closed the door and locked it again.

"Where's Lord Girlypanties — the wuss?" Pete glanced back at Elric and Francois. "Okay, the *other* wuss. Bertrand? Surely he wasn't the only one of us with enough sense to leave town."

"Bertrand's dead," Carmella answered. She was wearing yet another of those boob-hefting corset things she loved so much and Pete found it impossible to lift his gaze to her face, even as she delivered the somber news. "Fitzgerald took his head off."

"And he wasn't a wuss," Elric added snottily.

"Aw, look —" Pete turned away from the boob-spillage to look at the delicate vampire on the couch. "I'm sorry he's dead, but come on, he was totally a wuss." He turned back to find Carmella frowning at him. "And I say that in the most respectful way, of course."

"What are you doing here? I thought you left town," Carmella said.

Pete hesitated, unsure of where to begin. "All right, I know this sounds crazy, especially coming from me — but we've gotta get together on this thing. Take the fight to Fitzgerald."

The room was silent for a long moment, then Carmella spoke up: "I beg to differ, Pete — that would sound crazy coming from *anyone*."

"You want us all to get killed?" Pinball said.

"No, I want us all to kill *him*."

Elric sniffed. "You're the most retarded vampire ever."

Pete fixed the wispy creature with a sincere look. "I actually kind of take that as a compliment."

Sneering, Elric sat up, holding his spindly arms in front of himself like an effete praying mantis. "As it turns out, I have a much better idea. One that will solve this whole problem."

Pete swapped a look with Carmella and Pinball. They appeared to be just as surprised as he was. "Let's hear it, then," Pete prodded.

"It's easy." Elric daintily tossed his hair back from his face. "We make more vampires." Smiling smugly, he looked from face to face, searching for the praise he knew was coming. When nobody said anything, he added "You know — for Fitzgerald."

"Aw jeez," Pete muttered.

Pinball rolled her eyes.

"What?" Elric asked, disheartened. "If we keep him supplied with new vampires to feed on, he'll leave us alone."

"*That's* your spectacular plan," Pete said. "And you don't think the idea of making new vampires might have occurred to Fitzgerald somewhere along the way?"

"Well, *I* think it's a good idea," Elric said sourly.

"Jesus." Pete shook his head. "You all know damn well if it was a simple case of sucking down the blood of any old vampire, Fitzgerald would be chompin' on new people every night, then stuffing 'em away in his basement for later. Obviously whatever screwed up the old man's plumbing means he's gotta feast on us — or at least on vampires who've been around for awhile."

Elric looked like he was about to cry. "So you think it's better to just stroll on into his house and offer ourselves up?"

"Exactly — kind of," Pete said. "Whatever he did to Bertrand, it was to make a point — he's willing to kill us if he has to. But that's not what he wants. He needs us alive — well, as alive as any of us actually are."

"We can still run," Pinball said.

"No," Pete said. "We can't. *I* can't. He'll hunt us all down, kill us off one by one if he has to, even if it means he gets sicker. He's a vindictive son of a bitch, trust me. He sent a vampire to attack me and Angie at my place last night —"

"Angie?" Pinball asked. "The chick from the shitty bar across the street?"

"How'd you know that?"

"And you wonder why *idiot* equals *Pete*," Pinball said. "I watched you drive off with her the other night. It's not like you made any effort to be sneaky about it."

Carmella eyed Pete curiously. "Are you gonna turn her?"

"No, of course not," he said.

"Pussy," Pinball hissed.

"Lemme finish, will you?" Pete frowned. "We got away and Fitzgerald came after us himself. He took Angie."

"So this isn't as much about us being a team as it is about you wanting us to help get her back," Carmella said.

"Little of both," Pete nodded, half expecting the vampires to simply stop discussing the matter and start kicking the crap out of him.

Elric leaned back on the couch again, annoyed. "What makes you think she's not dead already?"

Pete sighed heavily. "Because Fitzgerald will keep her alive so that I'll do exactly what I'm doing now: talk all of you into going with me to fight him."

Elric *hmf*ed pointedly. "You're not talking us into anything."

Carmella took a deep breath, her bosom swelling arrestingly. "We have to do it."

"Are you out of your goddamn mind?" Pinball asked, stunned. "I don't know what the hell's up with Pete and his little girlfriend, but all of us —" her muscular arm swung around to indicate the other vampires, very nearly clothes-lining Pete in the process — "We have *lives* here."

"Then we need to fight for them," Carmella said, voice

steady. "I don't wanna die any more than I want to end up being Fitzgerald's living protein shake, but if we don't do *something*, the lives we have are over anyway. We can't stay here, and if we run, we'll be looking over our shoulders every minute of every day — shit, we're *already* doing that."

Carmella looked at Pete for his take. "Hey, keep talkin'," he said. "You're doing a better job than I was."

"You just said he *wants* us to come to him," Elric pointed out. "What makes you think we stand any chance at all of killing him?"

"Because he's arrogant," Pete said. "He thinks we're gonna be so scared of him that we'll cave as soon as he makes a move — or that if we do put up a fight, he'll have no trouble slaughtering us."

Elric's lips crinkled in a fretful pout. "Why does that *not* sound like a good reason to go along with this?"

"All right — I'm in," Pinball said. "Anything's better than sitting around waiting to get our heads chopped off."

"I don't know that I agree with that," Elric said. "And now I'm gonna look like the chickenshit if I back out."

"Then don't back out," Pete suggested.

Elric stared imploringly at Carmella for a moment, hoping he could will her to change her mind. When that didn't work, he hung his head sadly, chalky hair falling in his face. "All right," he said peevishly. "I'll go."

Slightly astonished that things were going so well, Pete nodded toward Francois le Sanguine. "You haven't had much to say, Francois le… Steve. You in?"

"Nuh-uh." Francois shook his head and took a deep drag on his smelly cigarette, showily blowing the smoke through his nostrils. "Fitzgerald didn't even turn me — Bertrand bit me and he's dead, so I'd say this isn't my fight."

"You're little and girlish anyway," Pete said, giving him a dismissive wave.

"Here's something that might be important," Pinball said. "How the hell are we supposed to *find* Fitzgerald and your little sweetiepie?"

"It's… taken care of." Pete looked vaguely uncomfortable. "I stayed at his house for awhile after he turned me."

Pinball's eyebrows went up. She and Carmella swapped a look.

"It's not like we were *dating*," Pete hastily added. "All right, question is — how do a bunch of vampires carry the crosses and shit that we're gonna need to fight a stronger and meaner vampire?"

34

Carmella's old Cadillac hearse rumbled and growled as it wound through the curves on its way up into the Hollywood Hills. The hearse's 472 cubic inch V8 had a hell of a lot of power, but it didn't like the constant slowing and speeding up Carmella was asking of it, and she'd killed the engine once already. As a result, she was taking it easy on the old beast, driving at a painfully slow rate of speed.

"I could just get out and walk next to the car, if it would help," Pete said, looking over at Carmella. She shot him a *feel-free-to-step-out-anytime* look.

Elric and Pinball were in the backseat, Mr. Stovall wedged between them. His vampire-hunting bag rested in his lap, its colorful smiley faces belying his incredible unease. On the floor between his feet was a black leather satchel, about two feet long, with worn leather handles.

The old man looked nervously at Pinball. She glowered at him, not very keen on the idea of bringing a human — especially one who owned a vampire-killing kit — along on the mission. Mr. Stovall turned to look at Elric, who smiled at him, deliberately exposing his fangs in the process.

Mr. Stovall leaned forward a bit, gently tapping Pete on the shoulder to get his attention. "If I get turned into a vampire, my wife's going to have something to say about it," the old man whispered.

"You'll be fine, Mr. Stovall," Pete said.

Not entirely convinced, Mr. Stovall eased back in his seat. Elric patted him reassuringly on the leg, giving him that fanged smile once again.

Earlier that evening, Mr. and Mrs. Stovall had been sitting on their couch, watching a rerun of *CSI*. Mr. Stovall wasn't a big fan of the series, largely because he knew Mrs. Stovall had a thing for the show's star, William Petersen ("If you were dead, I'd go to bed with that man," she'd once told him). He was very happy when Petersen left the show, but the damn thing was on constantly in reruns. It was like having the Other Man living in his television.

And on the matter of crime scene investigations, Mr. Stovall felt he'd done a fine job of handling the police after the ruckus at Pete's apartment the night before. Hoping to throw them off the trail, he'd told the officers that Pete had left with his young lady shortly before two rather beefy fellows with tattoos and fists like canned hams — wrestlers, from the look of them — had stormed into the apartment complex, yelling something about being on a crime spree, and that they were choosing their victims at random. The men had kicked their way through Pete's door and thrown various items around, apparently leaving when they found nothing of value. As for Pete, he and his girlfriend were out of town for a few days and Mr. Stovall didn't know how to contact them. The officers seemed a bit dubious about his story, feeling it was somewhat unusual for criminals to publicly announce their criminal plans while in the act, but Mr. Stovall stood by his tale, and soon afterwards, the cops wrapped up the scene and went on their way.

When the knock came at the door, he'd been happy for an excuse to walk away from William Petersen and his woman-thieving good looks, but as he shuffled across the living room, Mr. Stovall began to fear the police had seen through his lie and returned to take him in. He was, therefore, relieved to find Pete and his vampire friends standing in the hallway. When Pete explained what had happened — and that Angie had been kidnapped — Mr. Stovall didn't hesitate in agreeing to help them however he could. It was only when he was in the hearse with vampires all around him — heading for the home of another (and apparently less friendly) vampire — that he started to sweat a little. Shit, as the youngsters liked to say, was getting real.

Pete pointed at a side road coming up. "That's it — left, left."

Carmella slowed down even more — a feat Pete would've thought impossible — and cranked the hearse's hefty steering wheel, guiding the car onto Durand Drive. The engine lugged a bit as the hearse headed up the steep incline.

"Maybe this car's different," Pete said, ducking his head to look under the dash at Carmella's feet, "but there should be a pedal down there that sends fuel to the engine."

"Shut up."

His right foot shoving an invisible gas pedal to the floor, Pete sank back in his seat, frustrated and worried. Angie was up there right now, in Fitzgerald's house, suffering God knows what and surely scared half out of her mind — the last thing she needed was a rescue team chauffeured by a vampire who drove like old people screw.

Of course, that was assuming he was right about Fitzgerald's motives and Angie really was still alive.

Pete's foot pressed harder on the invisible gas pedal.

35

After what seemed like the longest drive in human (or vampire) history, the hearse finally rounded the last curve and topped the hill near Fitzgerald's house.

"That's it, this is it!" Frantic, Pete pointed at the old Spanish Colonial up ahead. "Pull over, here here here!" His finger thumped against the window as he indicated a little pull-off on the side of the road.

Carmella guided the big car off into the dirt, an area normally used to turn around on the narrow road. It wasn't quite large enough for the hearse but she was able to get most of the car off the blacktop and out of traffic, should any happen by. Pete had his door open and was out before the hearse stopped moving. He ran to the front of the vehicle, ducking down behind the fender and peering over the hood at the house.

Carmella and the other vampires got out, gazing down

the road in the direction Pete was staring. Stretching in such a way that her already-overflowing breasts nearly escaped their corral, Carmella walked around the front of the car.

"What are you doing?" Pete whispered. "Get down!"

"Okay, Jesus," Carmella said, hunkering down behind the fender next to Pete.

Pinball hustled around the back of the hearse, joining Elric alongside Pete and Carmella. "Which one is it?" Pinball asked.

"Third one up, on the left," Pete said. Glancing back, he noticed Mr. Stovall was still seated in the hearse. "Mr. Stovall! C'mon."

The old man leaned to his right, his face appearing in the space between the car's frame and the open back door. "I'm fine, I'll keep an eye on the car."

"No — we need you with us," Pete said. "That's the whole point."

"Ah, really?" Mr. Stovall pursed his wrinkled lips. "Because I don't mind staying here."

"Outta the car, old man," Pinball insisted.

Grumping under his breath, Mr. Stovall hefted the black leather satchel and dropped it on the ground outside, then planted his feet next to it. Gripping the car's frame, he groaned loudly and hoisted himself from the back seat, wobbling as he stood.

"We're also trying to be reasonably sneaky, Mr. Stovall," Pete said. "A little less noise would be great."

Frowning, Mr. Stovall gave Pete a quick salute, then groaned once more, this time at lower volume.

Pete stared at the house, eyes narrowed. *Son of a bitch* but he wasn't ready for this. "You guys ready?" he said, inadvertently looking directly at Carmella's chest.

"Are you speaking to vampires or tits?" she asked.

"Sorry — it's — they're just *right there* all the time," Pete said. "Let's go."

Awkwardly, Pete half-stood, assuming the universal sneaking-up-on-a-house posture and moving away from the hearse. As he crept out into the road, Carmella followed, Pinball and Elric close behind.

"Hell," Mr. Stovall muttered, watching the vampires make their way across the street. Slinging the smiley-face bag over his shoulder, he bent to grab the handles on the satchel. With a pained sigh, he straightened, wobbled a bit more, then shuffled off after the others.

Dashing the last few yards across the road, Pete took cover behind some Magnolia bushes. The other vampires quickly caught up with him and they all peered up at Fitzgerald's house again, waiting for Mr. Stovall.

"I just had a thought," Pinball whispered to Pete. "When did you get bit?"

"1973," Pete said. "Why?"

"And that was when you were Fitzgerald's houseboy?"

"It was when I lived in the house, yes," Pete answered, irritated.

"You weren't here like, last week or anything?"

"No."

"What if he moved?"

The expression on Pete's face may have given one the impression that he hadn't actually considered such a thing.

"I'm just sayin', 'cause that was almost forty freakin' years ago," Pinball continued. "And I only bring it up since, y'know, a bunch of vampires come bustin' in on some nice doctor and his family while they're watching TV, it's gonna be a little hard to explain."

Fuck, Pete thought.

"You seriously didn't think of that?" Carmella said.

"Let's just leave," Elric suggested.

"Nobody's goin' anywhere," Pete barked. "C'mon, look at that place — it's spooky as hell."

"Not for nothing," Carmella began, "but this discussion isn't giving me much confidence in our ability to kill Fitzgerald."

Pete huffed out a breath, fed up. "Look, we're here, all right? If we get inside and find Linda Ronstadt or somebody, then we'll just leave."

"Linda Ronstadt?" Mr. Stovall said, perking up.

"If she's here, you can stay," Pete offered. "But can we please just do this now, for Christ's sake?"

Shaking her head, Carmella gestured for Pete to lead on. Staying low, he darted out from behind the bushes and ran towards Fitzgerald's house. Carmella, Pinball and Elric followed, a bit half-heartedly this time, but there was a pronounced spring in Mr. Stovall's step, thanks to the possibility of surprising Ms. Ronstadt.

God damn me, Pete swore to himself as he moved up on the house. *I suck at everything*. He was terrible at being a vampire, terrible at being a boyfriend, and obviously worse than terrible when it came to rescuing the woman he loved.

Holy shit. It had been so long since he'd even thought about the possibility, he'd forgotten what the hell it felt like when it actually happened — but yeah, he was in love with Angie, as weird as it was to admit it to himself.

"How we goin' in here," Pinball whispered. "Through the windows, Manson Family-style?"

Pausing, Pete glanced over his shoulder at her. "Well, since there's been some concern expressed in regards to the notion that Fitzgerald might not actually live here anymore, I figured we should try the door first. Seems more polite."

"We're just gonna go up there and knock?" Elric asked, looking fearfully towards the house.

"You guys keep acting like I had time to think about all this," Pete said.

"Hey, dumbass," Pinball hissed. "We thought you *did* think about all this."

"If someone has a better plan, I'm happy to hear it." When none of the others offered anything, Pete begin moving along the walkway towards the front door again.

Was this easier for Carmella and the others, Pete wondered — were they gonna be better in the fight? After all, they were in it for the sake of their own skins, and that was one hell of a strong motivator. If Pete had learned anything about himself over the last couple of days, it was that he didn't really give a damn about his own skin if it meant living in a world that didn't include Angie. All he cared about was getting her out of this mess. If Fitzgerald managed to gain the upper hand, Pete knew he'd agree to whatever the vampire asked of him, on the condition that he let Angie go. Even if it meant never seeing her again.

Trying to put it out of his mind, Pete crept the last few yards to the entryway and the ostentatious double doors of the house. The other vampires were right behind him, Mr. Stovall bringing up the rear. Pete stared at the doors, hesitant. Even after so many years, the house terrified him — and made him furious. His stomach twisted at the memory of his days here all those years ago, learning what he'd been turned into.

And the awful things he did afterwards.

"Pete," Mr. Stovall whispered, snapping him out of it.

"Can we talk for a minute?"

Grateful for the reprieve, Pete nodded at the old man and the two stepped aside from the others. "What is it?"

Voice quavering slightly, Mr. Stovall fixed Pete with his old man's eyes. "I lied about my age, tried to join the army back in World War II. I was fourteen. They chased me out of the recruiting center, so I went to two more, tried the same thing. Couldn't get in."

"Mr. Stovall, I —"

"This is going somewhere, I'm not done," Mr. Stovall said, cutting Pete off. "When Korea came around, I was old enough, joined up. Saw things I don't like to think about, and made it through okay..." The old man drew a deep breath. "I don't want anything to happen to your girl, son. But I don't know I've got the sack for this. I get confused sometimes, too. Forget things. Go out to walk around the block, find myself three miles from home with no recollection how I got there. I don't know what I'm doing half the time, to be honest." He shook his head, embarrassed. "I'm saying, I don't want to mess things up in here."

If things went to hell, Pete would amend that deal with Fitzgerald: anything the bastard wanted from Pete, in exchange for Angie *and* the old man going free. "Mr. Stovall, you left your comfortable apartment to go off with a carload of vampires," Pete said, glancing at Carmella, Pinball and Elric. "One of them in velvet pants. I'd say you've got more sack than most people, including me. If I knew anybody else, I sure as hell wouldn't ask you to risk doing this — but we're going into a fight where we can't even hold some of the weapons we need. You're all we've got, and I'm honored to have you with us."

Mr. Stovall's face brightened, a wry smile playing across

his lips. "I can't promise I won't soil my trousers in here," he said.

"You and me both." Pete extended a hand. Mr. Stovall gripped it tight and they shook on the matter of potential pants-shitting, then rejoined the other vampires at the door.

"Man, right when you guys were about to start kissing," Pinball said.

Mr. Stovall made a smoochy-face at Pinball and walked past all of them to the front doors. He looked back at the vampires. "Fingers crossed for Linda Ronstadt," he whispered, then turned the knob.

Unlocked. Nervously, Mr. Stovall pushed the door open slightly. Pete and the other vampires stepped up behind the old man, all of them peering inside. At least as far as the entryway went, the coast was clear. Pete pushed the door open wide and stepped in, memories flooding through him as he entered the house for the first time in nearly forty years. Carmella walked in behind him, followed by Pinball, Mr. Stovall, and finally Elric, who looked as if he might be in the process of crapping his own plush velvet britches.

The team of vampire-hunting vampires moved quietly into the foyer, lit by the lamp on the Victorian table against one wall. About ten feet back from the front door, a narrow staircase wound upwards to the second floor, where a light burned softly. At the far end of the foyer was a closed door. Near the staircase was another doorway, this one open. Pete crept towards it, keeping an eye on the second floor.

Elric looked around the foyer, seemingly disappointed by Fitzgerald's decor — not nearly flamboyant enough, if you asked him. Boring old paintings and antiques. Movement caught his eye and he gasped girlishly.

Pete spun towards the sound. "What is it?" he whispered.

"Eww," Elric said, thrusting a slender finger towards the decorative ledge running the length of the foyer, just below the ceiling. A large rat scurried along the ledge, glaring down at the vampires with baleful red eyes.

"I don't think Linda Ronstadt would have rats," Mr. Stovall said.

Elric threw his bony arms wide above his head, his flouncy sleeves flapping. "Shoo! Shoo!"

The rat responded by leaping at Elric, landing on his head. Shrieking, Elric frantically danced around the foyer, batting and slapping at the creature tangled in his hair.

"For the love of —" Pete rushed towards the pathetic, wailing vampire. Darting in close, Pete threw a punch at Elric's head, clocking him a good one but dislodging the rat from his hair.

"*Owwww*," Elric bleated.

As it dropped, the rat transformed.

"Jumpin' shitcakes!" Pinball hollered. She and Carmella scrambled back from the thing.

What hit the Spanish tile floor was part rat, part man and entirely huge, with thickly muscled arms and two-inch claws. Nude, the thing's pale, translucent skin was patchy with coarse fur. Thick saliva dribbled from its disgusting yellowed teeth, red eyes glistening and wet.

Snarling, the monster suddenly lunged sideways, slamming Pete into the wall and knocking the wind out of him. Rising to its full height — an easy six-and-a-half feet — the beast sprang at Elric. A little squeak blurted from Elric's throat as the monster's hand shot out, its clawed fingers tangling in his white hair and yanking him off the floor.

Pete struggled to regain his feet, watching as the monster pulled Elric in close, its foul breath in his face causing the terrified vampire to retch.

Five feet into the house and we're thoroughly screwed, Pete realized.

36

Fighting down panic, Mr. Stovall dug through his smiley-face bag, his fingers closing around cold, comforting metal. He yanked the cross from the bag, shoving it towards the massive half-man, half-rat monstrosity. "Avast!" he scream-ed, voice quavering.

Pete and the other vampires recoiled instantly, howling and hissing and covering their eyes. The rat-thing, however, merely looked curiously at the old man, its fingers constrict-ing around Elric's throat, claws sinking into the vampire's pale flesh.

"For shit's sake, old man!" Pinball hollered, her muscled forearm shielding her face. "A little warning would be nice!"

"That's not gonna work," Pete yelled, back against the wall and peeking through his fingers at Mr. Stovall. "It's not a vampire!"

"Oh." Confused, Mr. Stovall continued to hold the cross out in front of himself.

"Put it AWAY!" Elric wailed, his voice rasping as the rat-thing continued to put the squeeze on his throat. Annoyed by Elric's shrieking, the monster slammed the frail vampire against the wall, hoping to shut him up but only causing him to squeak again.

Mr. Stovall shoved the cross back into the bag. Instantly, Pinball was on the move, ducking in low and driving a fist into the rat-thing's side, just below its bony ribs. Snarling, the creature released its grip on Elric, dropping him to the floor as it spun toward Pinball, swiping a clawed hand at her face. Springing away, she narrowly avoided the attack but tripped over her own feet and stumbled back into the table, knocking over the lamp. Both Pinball and lamp hit the floor at the same time, the lamp shattering, the light winking out.

In the dim light filtering down from the second floor, Mr. Stovall could see the rat-thing stalking towards him, red eyes like fire in its skull. Out of nowhere, Pete shouldered into the monster, knocking it aside. The two hit the wall hard enough to crack the plaster. Pete dropped to the floor, the rat-thing coming down on all fours near him. Growling, the beast caught Pete's ankle in its right hand. In one swift move it was on its feet, violently whipping him up and into the wall again, sending broken chunks of plaster flying across the foyer.

From where she lay on the floor, Pinball could see through the open doorway near the base of the stairs. Something in there shimmered enticingly in the sparse light. Getting to her feet, she darted through the doorway just as the rat-thing swung Pete into the wall once again.

Pete *whoof*ed as his face connected with the plaster. Bright light flashed behind his eyeballs, pain shooting through his skull. He felt his eyebrow split, blood coursing over his face. Almost casually, the monster heaved him back for another swing, Pete's head and shoulders dragging across the tiled floor, leaving a streak of crimson.

Before the monster could follow through, Carmella cocked back on one leg and drove a kick into the small of the rat-thing's back, her heel gouging the sallow and veiny flesh. With a thick, wet growl, the rat-thing whirled towards Carmella, wielding Pete's flailing body like a club. Pete felt the back of his head impact the soft cushion of Carmella's breasts, heard the wind go out of her as she staggered backwards. Just as his head hit the wall a third time, Pete glimpsed Pinball running from that side room, clutching what appeared to be a large medieval axe — but surely that was just the excruciating pain and the multiple head wounds talking.

"Hey, douchecakes!' Pinball yelled, lunging at the monster.

The axe blade sank deep into the rat-thing's chest. Half-gurgling, half-snarling, the rat-thing dropped Pete, who landed on his head with a grunt before flopping face-down on the tile. The creature collapsed on its back across him, axe still buried in its rib cage. Suddenly kicking and twitching spastically, it transformed once again — this time into a sinewy, naked man. Then, as quickly as it began, the thrashing stopped and the man lay still.

Sprawled on the floor where the rat-thing had dropped him, Elric sat up, fussily adjusting his ruffled shirt. Mr. Stovall stepped up to the vampire, offering a hand.

"Sorry about the cross," Mr. Stovall said.

Smirking, Elric took the old man's hand, both of them groaning as Elric got to his feet. "No problem," Elric sniffed. "It's only like getting whacked by a fifty-foot-tall nun with a ruler the size of a Buick." The vampire twisted to peer back over his shoulder at his narrow ass, then brushed at the seat of his velvet pants, *tsk*ing softly.

Pinball crouched next to Pete, who was still on the floor, the dead man lying across him in a heap. She grinned. "You okay?"

Pete's eyes flicked up to meet hers. The split in his eyebrow was already stitching itself back together, new skin crawling its way up the wound. "Please tell me this guy's naked peener isn't resting on the back of my hand."

She tilted her head to get a better look. "I think that's the balls, mostly — but the tip is definitely nudging you."

"Gahhh." Pete yanked his hand from beneath the corpse and sat up. Without thinking, he thrust that very same hand toward Pinball, who recoiled, sneering. "C'mon," Pete said, impatient. "Help me up, wouldya?"

"Dude, you just had a mutant cock in that hand."

Sighing, Pete withdrew his tainted mitt, shoving the other hand out instead. "Wasn't *in* it, it was *on* it," he muttered as Pinball tugged him to his feet. He looked down at the heavy axe jutting from the dead man's chest. "Where the hell did you get that?"

Pinball gestured toward the doorway at the base of the stairs. "Whole room's full of that kinda stuff." She bent and gripped the axe handle, twisted it with a sickening crunch, then yanked it from the corpse's torso. Rising, she rested the axe against her beefy shoulder and fixed Pete with a matter-of-fact expression. "Vampires always have medieval shit around the house."

37

Closing his eyes, Carson Fitzgerald calmly leaned back in the Danish mid-century modern lounge chair, long fingers wrapping over the black walnut arms. The chair was wildly out of place amidst the rest of the house's decor, but the Victorian high-back chair was a bit too throne-like for Fitzgerald's taste; the lounge chair was far less ostentatious, not to mention much more comfortable.

He'd actually felt a jolt of pain when his familiar died — unexpected, that. It made sense, though: being linked to someone so strongly and for so many years, the disconnect had to be like losing a limb.

Fitzgerald sucked in a deep breath through his nose, releasing it through his mouth. Completely unnecessary, of course, but every now and then, the simple, human act of breathing helped to settle his mind. The sickness was eating away at him, hunger building to the point of agony.

Fitzgerald's eyes snapped open at a loud *thunk* from elsewhere in the house. A wry smile twisted his lips. He knew Pete wouldn't disappoint him.

Rattles, bangs, creaking floorboards. The vampires were on the move.

They were going to do some damage, these wayward children.

38

When the vampires weaponed up in the roomful of medieval shit, Pete had chosen a flail or morning star or something — whatever the hell it was called, it involved a spiked metal ball dangling from a chain on the end of a stick — but now he found himself eyeing Carmella's sword and regretting his decision. He'd grabbed the flail because it looked cool and he figured it required absolutely zero skill to whack someone with the thing, but it was a pain in the ass to carry without whacking himself in the process. He'd already banged the spiked ball into the side of his knee, then accidentally swung it into Pinball's thigh, resulting in her fist accidentally finding its way into his mushy belly. Now he held it slightly out in front of himself and at an angle, the business end dangling dangerously. Truthfully, the weapon made him feel like an idiot, but it wasn't as bad as the goofy little dagger Elric carried.

Partly because he had once lived in the house but mostly because of his choice in weaponry and his resulting tendency to injure those around him, the others had shoved Pete ahead a few steps, urging him to lead the way. They were moving down a long, poorly-lit hallway, headed towards complete darkness at the other end. Carmella was just behind Pete, to his left (trying to avoid the flail in his right hand), Pinball a step or two behind her, clutching the handle of her axe with both hands. Mr. Stovall and Elric were side-by-side behind Pinball, Elric nervously glancing back over his shoulder, his knuckles whiter than usual as he squeezed the hilt of his dagger.

The old man had opted not to arm himself, largely because he already had his hands full with the smiley-face bag and the leather satchel, and he figured a sword or club wouldn't be of much use to him, anyway. There was one thing he *could* use very badly at the moment, however. "Excuse me," Mr. Stovall whispered, slipping past Elric and trotting a bit to catch up to Pete.

Pete studied the old man as he came up next to him. "You okay, Mr. Stovall?"

Mr. Stovall leaned in close to Pete, speaking softly. "Is there a restroom?"

"Hitch up your Depends, old man," Pinball said.

"I'm sure we can find one," Pete said.

"Soon, I hope."

They walked in silence for a moment, then Pete had a thought. "Did you say *avast* back there?"

Mr. Stovall shrugged. "I don't know what's appropriate."

Up ahead, a loud, metallic *clunk* emanated from the darkness. Pete and the others froze, then —

Ka-chung choom choom choom choom CHUNK.

Earsplitting, grinding. As if something ancient and iron and frightening had crawled through the black.

Pete stared into the darkness at the end of the hallway, the darkness they were going to have to walk right the hell into, and he was scared beyond belief. Not for himself — for Angie. This place was a goddamned house of horrors, and he didn't even want to imagine what Angie might be going through. Maybe — just maybe — she was fortunate enough to be unconscious. If she wasn't… well, Pete hoped she realized he was coming for her, that he'd do anything to save her.

"Hey, snap out of it," Carmella whispered, nudging him. "What was that?"

Pete's flail suddenly felt even more useless. "I don't know."

"You lived here, asshole," Carmella snarled. "Try to be of some use."

"Hey, there wasn't any medieval shit or rat monsters or terrifying sounds at the end of the hallway back then," Pete said, gesturing dangerously with the spiked flail. "The whole place kinda looked like the cover of *Yellow Submarine*, actually."

"Really?" Elric asked. "I would've thought more like *Sabbath Bloody Sabbath* or Deep Purple's third album."

"No, Fitzgerald had this psychedelic thing going on —" Pete's voice trailed off and he cocked an eyebrow at the wimpy vampire. "I wouldn't have made you for a Sabbath fan, Elric."

Pleased with himself, Elric made a tiny theatrical bow, arms spread.

"Way to spoil the moment," Pete said.

"Jesus, what the fuck is wrong with you two?" Pinball gestured towards the darkness ahead with the blade of her axe. "For all we know, the friggin' gates of Hell just opened up and you're yammerin' like a couple of ninety-year-old metalheads."

"Tell 'em to hitch up *their* Depends," Mr. Stovall snickered.

"Shut up, idiots," Carmella said, pointing with her sword. "Look."

Pete and the others peered into the black. A pair of eyes, glowing with pale fire, hung in the shadows. The eyes blinked, opened again —

And were joined by a second pair. Then another.

"Oh shit," Pete whispered. He tested the heft of his flail, wishing once again that he'd gone for a sword. Or even a cinderblock. At least he probably wouldn't hit himself with a cinderblock.

As two more sets of eyes appeared in the darkness, a hellish glow began to rise, silhouetting five rather curvaceous figures standing just inside a sunken room at the end of the hall. The edge of a heavy metal door could be seen on one side of the hall, where it had slid — with accompanying racket — back into a recess.

"Gates of Hell my ass," Pete said. "That was the door to the ladies' room opening."

The lighting in the room reached a spookshow level of creepiness. A smoky haze, stinking of incense, drifted throughout the room and into the hallway. Three stone steps led down to the floor, which was entirely covered with what looked like thick shag carpet and piled with the vampire equivalent of throw pillows and bean bag chairs. Silken drapes adorned the walls.

The ladies in question looked a lot like Suzanne had when she smashed her way into Pete's apartment — eyes sunken and crazed, skin sickeningly gray, hair wild.

"Hippies," Mr. Stovall said.

"Worse," Pete said. "Vampire brides."

The women were all clad in filmy, low-cut nightgowns, plentiful cleavage prominently displayed. With their anemic flesh and dead eyes, it was nearly impossible to tell one from the other, outside of their hair color, and even that was filthy and dull. Two of the women were cobweb-blonde, the others sporting snarls of long black hair that encircled their pallid faces. A couple of them made odd purring sounds, the tips of their fangs showing.

"I realize I'm in no position to throw stones," Carmella said, her own cleavage bobbling spectacularly with every word, "but, c'mon — the *boobs*. It's almost embarrassing."

"What is this, Fitzgerald's love den?" Pinball asked.

"I think it's more like the snack bar," Pete said. "Look at 'em — he's obviously been feeding on them."

Elric perked up at that. "Then my idea to make more vampires *was* a good one — he's already been doing it!"

"We've been over this — it was a *great* idea except for the part about it not really working." Pete took a couple hesitant steps forward, watching the brides closely.

"Should I get the cross out?" Mr. Stovall stuck his hand into the smiley-face bag.

"No," Carmella said.

"Let's just hang loose on the cross for now, Mr. Stovall." Pete put a hand on the old man's arm to prevent any religious-artifact misfires. Glancing back, Pete noticed the other vampires hadn't moved forward with him. "Hey — pick up the pace, assholes. I'm not goin' in there alone."

Pete waited until Pinball, Carmella and Elric caught up to him, then began slowly moving forward again. Pinball watched Mr. Stovall as the old man stuck close to Pete, his hands trembling slightly on his vampire-slaying kit.

"I just realized who you remind me of, Stovall," the muscular vampire whispered, grinning. "Don Knotts."

Mr. Stovall shot an annoyed look back at her. "What?"

"Yeah. In *The Ghost and Mr. Chicken*."

"Don't make me get my cross out," Mr. Stovall warned.

"Don't make me hit you with my axe," Pinball said.

Elric nodded towards the vampire brides. "What are they doing?"

The women had begun slowly backing further into the sunken room, writhing and squirming in an exaggerated manner, their bony hands beckoning, lips pouting seductively. All five of them were making that odd purring sound now.

"I'm pretty sure they're workin' the come-hither thing," Pete said.

Pinball sneered. "Yuck."

Pete paused at the top of the steps leading down into the

sunken room, the other vampires closing ranks behind him. The vampire brides continued cooing and purring, a couple of them aggressively fondling themselves, their excitement growing as Pete and the others got closer.

Pinball nudged him with her elbow. "What are you waitin' for?"

Pete was staring at the edge of the massive metal door where it was visible in the wall. "What if we get down there and this door closes behind us?" Pete looked back at his little crew of vampire-slayers. It was obvious none of them were very pleased with that notion, but there didn't seem to be much choice. His gaze settled on Pinball. "Maybe we should leave your axe here to wedge it open. Just in case."

"Not a fuckin' chance," Pinball growled, her fingers tightening around the axe handle.

"Look — we're all vampires, right?" Elric chirped.

"No," Mr. Stovall said.

Ignoring the old man, Elric continued. "Maybe we can just… talk this out. Especially if Fitzgerald's feeding on them." He gestured with his thin fingers towards the roomful of vampire brides. "If we can make them understand that we're here to kill Fitzgerald —"

Sudden, insane shrieking interrupted Elric's plan for vampire detente as the nearest bride — one of the blondes — launched herself at Pete, fangs bared in fury.

"Whoa!" Pete hollered, awkwardly ducking to the side and swinging his flail in the same movement. The spiked ball missed the airborne bride entirely, snapping back as it hit the end of its chain and cracking Pete in the forehead. Grunting, he lost his footing and tumbled down the stone steps.

* * *

Pinball saw Pete hit himself with the mace or whatever the hell it was, but missed seeing him fall into the love den — her eyes were glued to the blonde. The bride hit the hallway wall, hung there for a second, then scurried along like a crab over the heads of Pinball and the others. With a snarl, Pinball swung her axe, the blade chiseling into the plaster wall and pinning the tail of the bride's nightgown. Glowering at Pinball, the bride hissed angrily but kept right on going, tearing the nightgown loose. She dropped to the floor behind Pinball and the vampire hit squad, aiming to cut off any retreat.

A piercing wail sounded right next to Pinball's left ear as Elric screamed, stabbing the air with that stupid dagger of his as he stumbled backwards and nearly fell over Mr. Stovall. Her bouncer sensibilities kicking in, Pinball quickly assessed the situation: the blonde bride was holding her ground, not attacking. Pinball had no doubt the bride would make a move given the chance, but at the moment she was just running interference. The real danger was from the four other brides still in the sunken room.

Glancing back over her shoulder, Pinball saw the remaining brides rush forward, drooling and screaming, gnarled claw-like hands clutching at the air. Carmella dashed down the steps, sword at the ready, only to trip over Pete as he pushed himself to his feet. Amazingly, Carmella caught her balance and came back up, slashing upwards with her sword at the same time. The blade opened a diagonal slash across the torso of the closest bride, one of the ratty dark-haired chicks. Meanwhile, still in the hallway, Elric was squawking and thrusting ineffectually with his dagger, trying to hide behind Mr. Stovall, who cowered off to one side.

Jesus, Pinball thought. It was like watching that awesome battle with the cave troll in *The Fellowship of the Ring* if the Hobbits and Dwarves and Elves had all been a bunch of awkward spazzes.

Gripping her axe firmly, Pinball savored the feel of the ancient leather handle biting into her palms. *Goddamned if a bunch of half-naked vampire bitches are gonna be the end of me.* Shouldering past Elric, she leapt into the action.

* * *

Pete dabbed at his forehead, feeling the fresh skin forming over the puncture wounds he'd inflicted on himself with the flail. As he rose, somebody ran headlong into him, knocking him down again. He caught a glimpse of flashing steel, then realized it was Carmella. Her sword opened one of the brides from right hip to left breast. The mindless vampire shrieked in pain, leaping — no, *floating* back several feet, hanging there above the floor as if she were on wires. *What the hell*, Pete thought. *Did I miss a week of vampire school or something?* He stared dumbfounded as the vampire chick hovered over the sea of throw pillows, the ugly slash on her torso already healing.

Pete felt a breeze ruffle his curly mop as Pinball sailed over his head. She swung her heavy axe in mid-air, the blade narrowly missing the injured bride. Pinball was already drawing back for another swing as her boots hit the floor. At least she wasn't floating around like a big ol' balloon, too. Must have missed the same vampire class.

Considering all he'd done so far was get smacked into a

wall — repeatedly — by a giant rat, then hit himself in the head and fall down some steps, Pete was beginning to feel a bit like he wasn't contributing much to the mission. Extricating himself from the nest of pillows on the floor, he sprang to his feet, only to find himself directly in the path of Carmella's sword as she slashed at the second blonde bride. Yelping, Pete leapt back, dodging the blade. He hit the floor, saw Blondie circling Carmella and coming his way, and instinctively lashed out with the flail. The spiked ball hit the back of the vampire's head with a soft thud and stuck there. Hissing, Blondie spun towards Pete, yanking the flail from his grip, the wooden handle and chain dangling from her scalp like a medieval hair extension. As she made a grab at Pete, Carmella's sword cut neatly through her neck. Eerily, Blondie's eyes remained focused on Pete as her severed head flew past him, landing in the hallway with a wet *thwack*.

* * *

Mr. Stovall jumped back against the wall as the vampire's head rolled towards him, the flail's handle clattering on the tile, blood whipping around from the stump of her neck like a garden sprinkler and spattering his Hush Puppies.

Holy Jesus, these things are real. Fighting the urge to pull the cross from his bag, he kicked at the severed head, knocking it down into the sunken room. Behind him, Elric was whimpering and stabbing his tiny knife in the general direction of the busty blonde vampire. The poor guy probably thought he was keeping the vampire at bay, but it seemed obvious to Mr. Stovall that she was just hanging back to make sure they didn't run out the way they came in.

Returning his attention to the fight, Mr. Stovall wondered if Pete and the others had spotted the door in the far wall, partially hidden by the fluttering drapery.

Avoiding Elric's wild thrashing, Mr. Stovall clutched his vampire-slaying bags tightly and ran for the steps, slipping a bit in the slick blood that covered the hall floor. Pausing at the top of the steps, he stared down at the bizarre scene: a headless corpse sprawled among the throw pillows, the masculine vampire girl heaving a big axe around like she knew what she was doing, the vampire girl with the rack that wouldn't quit swinging a sword like it was a baseball bat, and his quiet neighbor Pete, standing there empty-handed as a bunch of vampire floozies tried to kill them all.

Mr. Stovall hadn't even believed in vampires before a few months ago — not until he was standing on the front steps of the apartment building one night, chatting with Pete. Something had felt wrong about the whole scenario — he couldn't put his finger on what the hell it was, but he felt like his skin was trying to crawl off his body. Then it hit him: he was staring at his own reflection in one of the front windows, but there was no sign of Pete's. Thinking it was a trick of the light or the angle he was at, Mr. Stovall shuffled back and forth, trying to force Pete's reflection to appear. Nothing. He could look at the guy right there in front of him, reach out and poke him, but he cast no reflection. Suddenly feeling like he might throw up, Mr. Stovall had excused himself and hurried inside, unable to accept what he'd seen. He'd started keeping tabs on Pete's comings and goings after that, and it didn't take a genius to figure out that he was no ordinary neighbor. Even still, Mr. Stovall didn't want to accept that vampires could actually exist — but here he was in a nest of the damn things.

Screwing up his courage, Mr. Stovall carefully picked his way down the steps — his shoes were slippery with blood, after all — and hoped like hell he'd get to see his wife again.

* * *

Carmella's hand was sweaty on the sword's hilt. She was glad she hadn't picked a useless weapon like Pete's flail, but she didn't know how to use the sword — she'd never even held one before, outside of the wooden toy she'd played with as a child. She was just wildly swinging the thing and hoping to do some damage. She wanted to switch the sword to her left hand, wipe the sweat from her right, but with two of the brides closing in on her, that didn't seem like a good idea. And the bride she'd sliced open looked pretty well pissed about it, too.

From the corner of her eye, she saw Pinball's axe slice past the third bride, the one with the mole at the top of her cleavage, like she'd been eating chocolate chip cookies and a tiny bit had gotten away. Hissing, the bride shot straight up in the air, hitting the ceiling and clinging to it like a spider.

As Carmella tilted her head to follow Ms. Chocolate Chip, one of the other brides lunged for her. Startled, Carmella whipped the sword around, the tip slicing into the meaty part of the bride's forearm. She felt the hilt slip in her sweaty hand, but maintained her hold on it. As she drew back for another swing, a spray of blood suddenly hit Carmella in the face. Blinking it off, she saw Pinball's axe buried in the bride's head, cleaving it through at an horrific angle. Her head falling open like a split lobster, the bride jerked a bit, then went limp.

"Didn't mean to get that on you," Pinball yelled,

wrenching the axe loose from the sagging body.

Carmella wiped at the blood on her face. Then Ms. Chocolate Chip dropped on Carmella's back from above, sinking her fangs into Carmella's neck.

* * *

Upon seeing another one of her sisters die, the blonde bride blocking their escape route snarled hatefully and rushed at Elric. Letting loose with a battle cry that sounded very much like a prairie dog yipping in a field, he drove forward with his Elvish dagger, but amazingly, the bride seemed unafraid of him or his weapon. Just as Elric realized it might be a good idea to flee, her claw-like hands closed around his upper arms, ragged nails tearing through his shirt sleeves and into the pale flesh beneath. Scared as he was, he still had the sense to hope the others didn't realize the high-pitched scream echoing through the hallway was coming out of him. The bride lifted the kicking, writhing vampire to shoulder level — there wasn't a lot of weight involved in Elric's construction — and angrily hurled him away. Elric hit the floor at the end of the hall, his velvet pants sliding easily on the tile, then skidded through the pool of blood and dropped down the steps to land between Mr. Stovall and Pete, where he was swallowed up by the comfy throw pillows scattered about Fitzgerald's love den. Prodding gingerly at his crotch, Elric was grateful to discover he hadn't wet his pants.

* * *

Ignoring Elric, who seemed to be mating with the pillows on the floor near his feet, Pete thrust a hand towards Mr. Stovall, shouting "Stake stake *STAKE!*"

The old man didn't move, mesmerized by the sight of the vampire bride clinging to Carmella's back, blood oozing from her neck where the bride's fangs were sunk into the flesh.

"*Come on!*" Frustrated, Pete stomped across Elric's bony ass and jammed his hand into Mr. Stovall's smiley-face bag, fishing around.

"Hey, ow!" Elric hollered.

Sudden, unbearable pain lit Pete up as his hand brushed against the metal cross, his skin instantly crisping. With a yell that made Elric feel a little better about his own girlish shrieking, Pete jerked his hand from the bag, cradling it in the other. Tears streamed from his eyes as he peered at the injury, a partial image of the cross seared into the fleshy part of his palm and up across the fingers.

Snapping out of it, Mr. Stovall fumbled with the bag, digging in and coming up with a sharpened wooden stake. As he handed it to Pete, the blonde bride from the hallway sailed overhead, taking the opportunity to swipe at Pete with her jagged fingernails. Pete dodged, his head snapping back just in time to see Pinball's axe blade drive into the blonde's left shoulder near the neck, the impact slamming the vampire to the floor. Quickly, Pinball stepped in and jammed a boot down on the blonde's back. Wresting the axe loose, Pinball raised it overhead, trailing gore, then brought it down again, this time slicing the blonde's head clean off. Screaming in rage, the third raven-haired bride flew at Pinball, only to take the vampire girl's fist directly in her blighted face.

Pete winced as something slapped into his burnt hand.

He looked down at the mallet, Mr. Stovall's hand still gripping the head of it. Closing his fingers over the handle, Pete shot a look of thanks at the old man, then ran to help Carmella.

Twisting and turning in an attempt to fling Ms. Chocolate Chip off her back, Carmella was inadvertently swinging her sword around like she was swatting flies. Pete ducked under the blade and darted in close just as Carmella spun towards him again, the sword whipping past his ear and nearly giving him a buzz-cut on that side of his head. Now face-to-face with Carmella, Pete gestured frantically. "Bend over! Now! NOW!"

Carmella shook her head, confused, then saw the stake and mallet in Pete's hands. She suddenly leaned forward at the waist, bracing her hands on her knees and putting the ferocious vampire bride right where Pete needed her.

Christ, I hope this doesn't go right through her, Pete thought as he jammed the sharpened point of the stake into the flesh of the bride's back. Realizing what was about to happen, Ms. Chocolate Chip tore her fangs loose from Carmella's neck, slinging blood and slobber everywhere as she snarled at Pete. Putting all his weight into it, he brought the mallet down, pounding the stake through the bride's back.

The bride's agonized scream very nearly drowned out Carmella's "*Fuck!*"

Pete's teeth ground together. *Yup, went right through her.* He stumbled away, watching as Ms. Chocolate Chip thrashed violently, then erupted into a cloud of smoke and ash. The stake remained in place, however, the tip sunk an inch into Carmella's back.

Dropping her sword, she reached back with both hands, slapping desperately at the stake. "Get it out, get it *out!*"

"Hold still!" With one hand on Carmella's shoulder, he took hold of the stake and tugged it free. Carmella grunted and fell to her knees, breathing hard. "Sorry," Pete said.

Still in too much pain to speak, Carmella lifted a hand, signaling the a-okay.

"Hey, you guys just relax, why don'tcha," Pinball said. "I've got this one." Axe poised to strike, she slowly circled the last vampire bride.

The creature's crazed expression was finally beginning to show a glimmer of something like fear. Suddenly, the bride launched herself towards the ceiling, where she'd be safely out of range. She shot upwards several feet, then stopped dead like a dog hitting the end of a leash. A stunned look crossed her face, becoming sheer terror as she looked down to see Pinball's hand closed around her ankle.

Pinball smiled. With a violent jerk, she brutally slammed the bride down into the nest of pillows. Pinball's boot came down on the small of her back. She screamed, struggling frantically, then everything went silent as Pinball buried the axe in the bride's head and into a pillow beneath, sending up a mushroom cloud of blood and feathers.

"And that, I believe," Pinball said, tugging the axe loose and turning towards the others, "is *that*."

39

Carmella wanted to take a breather, give her assorted wounds a few minutes to heal, but Pete wasn't having any of it. Angie was somewhere in the house and every obstacle

Fitzgerald threw in their path only gave him that much more time to do — well, God only knew what.

"You fucking *staked* me, man," Carmella griped.

"I said I was sorry." Pete was already heading for the door Mr. Stovall had found in the far wall, trying not to trip over all those goddamned pillows along the way.

Carmella sighed, then groaned theatrically as she bent to retrieve her sword.

"Forget it," Pete called back over his shoulder.

"Dammit," Carmella muttered. Seeing she wasn't going to get her way, she followed in Pete's wake through the pillows.

Pinball helped Elric up, shaking her head as she looked at his dagger. "Really man — why even bother?"

Elric examined the blade, turning it this way and that, then looked at Pinball, the tiniest bit of hurt in his eyes. "It's Elvish."

"That's what I'm saying," Pinball said, shoving him along behind Pete and the others.

Mr. Stovall was at the door kicking pillows out of the way as Pete walked up. He reached for the metal knob, then paused, contemplating. "Mr. Stovall — get that cross out."

"Whoaaaa," said Pinball, stopping in her tracks. The other vampires did the same, looking at Pete like he was out of his mind.

"Just cover your eyes and trust me," Pete said.

The vampires lifted their hands, shielding their eyes as Mr. Stovall reached into his smiley-face bag. As he extracted the cross, Pete yelped slightly.

"What?" Mr. Stovall asked, nervous.

"I kinda saw it," Pete said, his arm across his face. "My fault." With his free hand, he felt around for the doorknob, getting a grip on it. "Ready?"

Mr. Stovall nodded, then remembered Pete couldn't see him. "Go," he said, holding the cross tightly.

Pete pulled the door open and Mr. Stovall ducked through, brandishing the cross like a cop entering a crime scene.

"Clear," Mr. Stovall said, pleased with his use of the lingo. He tucked the cross back into the bag and the vampires lowered their arms.

Pete stood in the doorway. The narrow corridor beyond was the first part of the house that really looked like something from a horror movie: gray stone walls, cobwebs in the corners, the stink of ancient mold. The floor was also made of stone, but the two light fixtures — one at either end of the corridor — were only designed to look like antique candelabra: low-watt electric bulbs burned in both of them. Too much trouble to go around lighting candles all the time, no doubt.

It was also the first time Pete felt stirrings of familiarity since they'd entered the house. Now he remembered the sunken room — it had been decorated differently back in 1973, and the heavy metal door hadn't been there, but he knew where they were now. He nervously eyed the wooden door at the far end of the corridor, about forty feet away. There were no other doors along the walls. No place else to go.

Throwing the door wide open, Pete started down the corridor. Mr. Stovall stuck close to him, Pinball next. Carmella, not in any big hurry, gestured for Elric to go first, then brought up the rear.

As he moved along the familiar corridor, Pete tried to tell himself the brides and Fitzgerald's familiar were better off dead than living as mad things, doing the Master's bidding and providing him with a food source, but he still felt awful about killing them. Hell, there'd been plenty of times over the years where he figured he might as well wander out into the sunrise and get it over with — when going out in a cloud of ash seemed better than living the way he had been.

That was before he met Angie, though.

He glanced back at Pinball, marching along like freaking Conan the Barroom Brawler with that axe cocked against her shoulder. She didn't seem to be suffering any remorse, that was for certain. "Hey," he whispered to her. "The way those brides were flyin' and floatin' and all that — can you do that?"

"Nope," Pinball said.

"Me neither," Carmella whispered from the back of the crew.

Pete looked at Elric, who simply shrugged.

"What the hell, I wonder why none of us got that superpower," Pete said. "It would come in real handy at my job."

"Maybe it's somethin' we could do if we tried," Pinball said. "Let's face it, it's not like those chicks had anything better to do than sit around all day figurin' out what kinda vampire shit they're capable of. Kinda like dogs'll get bored and start tryin' to get out of the yard."

Carmella peered past the others, towards the wooden door at the end of the hall. "I swear this place is bigger on the inside than it is on the outside."

"Just wait," Pete said.

"Wonderful. I should've worn my comfortable vampire-slaying shoes."

As they approached the wooden door, Pete said "All right, let's do that cross thing again, Mr. Stovall."

"Aw man," Pinball said. "That thing hurts even when you're not lookin' at it."

Mr. Stovall stuck his hand into the bag once again as the vampires covered their eyes. Pete fumbled around for the doorknob, gripped it tight. Taking a deep breath, he opened the door, the wood scraping along the stone floor with a startling shriek.

Getting a little carried away, Mr. Stovall made a slight hop into the doorway, very nearly tripping and tumbling down the flight of stone steps that curved downwards into darkness.

"Ooo," Mr. Stovall said, steadying himself. "That's a lot of stairs."

"Put the cross away," Pete reminded the old man.

Mr. Stovall slid the cross back into his bag. Pete stepped to the edge of the stairs, peering down into the black. She had to be down there. He realized his knees were wobbling, just the tiniest bit. Hoping they couldn't tell how scared he was, he looked over his shoulder at the other vampires grouped in the doorway.

"Here we go."

40

Settling back in his chair, Fitzgerald steepled his fingers in front of his face, the tiniest smile tweaking the corners of his mouth despite the pain gnawing through his guts.

Here we go.

41

During the short time Pete had lived in Fitzgerald's house, he'd never ventured down that stone staircase. His room had been on the upper floor, and while he'd certainly been curious as to what the Master's lair might look like, it had been off-limits. The closest he'd ever come was the night he'd opened that wooden door at the top of the stairs and yelled down at Fitzgerald that he was leaving. Expecting a fight, Pete had almost felt disappointed when Fitzgerald didn't respond.

But good things come to those who wait, as somebody somewhere always says; Pete had no doubt he was going to get that fight now. As he led Mr. Stovall and the Vampire Trio down the dark staircase, Pete wondered what kind of scenario awaited them below. He'd barely had time to imagine the cobweb-draped Haunted Mansion they'd be facing when they reached the bottom of the stairs — spooky and dark though it was, the stone staircase was deceptively short, curving down only a single floor, where another closed wooden door stood in their path. Pete knew the third floor of the house only from the outside — running the length of the building, it jutted from the back, out over the sloping hillside, most of the structure propped up on stilts. There had been more than one occasion back in 1973 wherein Pete, unable to sleep, found himself riding out a minor earthquake and hoping it would dump Fitzgerald's private quarters down the hillside, spilling the vampire out into the bright sunlight.

Pete wasn't sure how long he'd been staring at that closed door at the bottom of the stairs when Mr. Stovall finally jarred him out of it.

"Want me to get the cross out again?"

Pete considered for a moment. "No."

"You sure about that?" Pinball asked. "If this is Fitzgerald's bedroom, maybe we should go in religious symbols blazin'."

"I don't wanna do anything that might... set him off," Pete said.

"You mean like breakin' into his house and killin' his girlfriends?"

Pete ignored Pinball's wiseass — but pretty much spot-on — comment. For some damn reason, he still had it in his head that this whole thing might end well, at least for Angie and Mr. Stovall, and banging through Fitzgerald's door into his private chambers and waving a cross around seemed like it might be detrimental towards that end.

Pete turned to face the would-be assault team: an eighty-year-old man, a vampire chick built like Franco Columbu, another vampire chick whose outrageous tits were about to rupture from her clothing, and a vampire dude who was more of a chick than the actual chicks. And Pete was very likely going to get them all killed. He shook his head, resigned. "Maybe I should just go in alone."

"I second that," Elric said, gesturing with his Elfin dagger.

"Shut up," Pinball told the skinny vampire. She eyed Pete with something that he might have taken for *respect*, had it come from anybody else. It made him a little uncomfortable, to be honest. "We didn't fight our way in here just to cool our heels while you take on the big man alone."

A little smile played across Pete's lips. "You talk like a comic book."

"You shut up, too," Pinball said. She shouldered her axe and nodded towards the door. "Let's get this shit underway."

Pete lifted his empty hands, wishing he had a baseball bat or a rolled up magazine or *something*. "Mr. Stovall, can I have that hammer?"

The old man started to dig into the smiley-face bag, then changed his mind. "Got something better," he said, grinning at Pete. Mr. Stovall's knees made the sound of bacon frying as he crouched, resting his leather satchel on the floor. Unzipping it, he smiled up at Pete again, then dug into the satchel.

"Whatta you got in there?" Pete asked, peering over the old man's shoulder.

"This is good, you'll like this." Mr. Stovall wrestled a small hand crossbow from the satchel, along with a thin wooden stake, the dull end fitted with plastic fins, like a lawn dart, and held them up proudly.

"Look at that, you got the little fins on it and everything." Pete watched as Mr. Stovall tapped his fingertip against the sharpened end of the stake. "Wait a minute, did you — were you plannin' on shootin' *me* with that thing?"

"Not now," Mr. Stovall said sheepishly. "Probably a little bit, before." His knees crackling and popping again, Mr. Stovall grunted his way to his feet. Resting the butt of the crossbow against his pot belly, the old man struggled to draw back the bowstring, his scrawny forearms quivering with the effort. Giving up, he handed the crossbow to Pete.

"Uhh," Pete said, turning the crossbow around in his hands, trying to develop a plan of attack. Finally settling on Mr. Stovall's approach, he braced the butt of the crossbow against his own doughy gut and tugged at the string, grunting softly. Arms trembling, he was able to pull the string a few inches back, but no further.

"Jesus," Pinball sneered. Leaning her axe against the wall, she took the crossbow from Pete and quite handily drew the string back, cocking it. She held the crossbow out, allowing Mr. Stovall to notch the stake as Pete stared on, embarrassed. "You a good enough shot?" Pinball asked Pete.

"Are you?"

She held his gaze for a moment, then handed the crossbow back to him. "Pressure's on, he-man." Pinball retrieved her axe as Pete nervously tested the heft of the crossbow.

"Just remember, point arrow away from face," Carmella said.

"It's fairly straightforward," Mr. Stovall added.

Annoyed, Pete stepped towards the door. "All right, I think I can figure it out — let's go." As his hand fell on the doorknob, Pete looked back at Mr. Stovall. "This might've been handy to have before we came through the front door, y'know."

"I've only got the one arrow," Mr. Stovall said.

"That is *spectacular*," Pete said. "Exactly what I needed to hear."

Taking a deep breath, Pete squeezed the doorknob. Pinball stepped up close behind him, axe at the ready. Behind Pinball, Carmella tried to angle her sword so as not to inadvertently stab anyone. Elric, as usual, brought up the rear — standing at the base of the stone steps, prepared to flee back up them should things go wrong when the door opened. Mr. Stovall was in the process of becoming one with the wall, just hoping he could stay out of the way.

Pete shot a look over his shoulder at Pinball. She gave him a nod, ready as she'd ever be. In one quick movement, Pete twisted the knob and lunged forward, pancaking against the unmoving door as Pinball and Carmella's momentum created a chain reaction vampire pile-up — not to mention one hell of a lot of racket.

Pete *huffed* softly as Pinball and Carmella peeled themselves off of him and stepped back. As the vampires regained their composure, the calm voice of Carson Fitzgerald came from within the closed room, saying one simple word: "Pull."

"Shit," Pete said, looking at the others. "I guess it's not like we really had the element of surprise going on anyway, right?"

"Whatever, super-genius," Pinball said. "Just open the fucking door."

Embarrassed, Pete turned the knob and pulled the door open. The first thing he saw was Angie, sprawled on the floor at Fitzgerald's feet, looking drugged or mesmerized or something, but definitely — gloriously — *alive*. And judging from what he could see of her neck, unbitten. Her head bobbed up slightly as Pete stepped into the room, looking towards him with what seemed a glimmer of recognition, and he felt like his heart was going to bust out of his chest and run around the room like a hideous monkey.

Pinball and Carmella followed Pete in, flanking him. Elric waited for Mr. Stovall to enter, then stepped in behind him, turning one last time to threaten the empty staircase with his tiny dagger.

The back wall of the room was about forty feet away

from where they stood, lined floor to ceiling with shelves, all of them packed to overflowing with books. The room ran about seventy or eighty feet side-to-side. Another rack of bookshelves stood at one end, while a dressing table and a Victorian sofa, upholstered in pale blue velvet, occupied the opposite wall. Off to the left of the door Pete and the others had come through, Fitzgerald's coffin stood perched atop a wooden pedestal, the lid open to reveal the immaculate cream-colored lining. The room was windowless except for a large segmented dome skylight, probably fifteen feet in diameter, in the center of the ceiling. Moonlight struggled against the haze of L.A. smog, filtering weakly through the glass. The only other light in the room came from a small lamp on the table next to Fitzgerald's lounge chair, where the vampire lord was seated, right foot propped atop his left knee, hands on the arms of the chair, staring calmly at the new arrivals. Angie deliriously gazed up from where she was draped at the foot of his chair. Not a cobweb, bat, spider or skull anywhere to be seen. Pete wasn't quite sure what he'd been expecting, but this looked like Frank Frazetta did the poster art for *My Fair Lady*.

Fitzgerald smiled broadly at Pete and the others. "Hello, children."

42

Angie heard someone speak, but the voice seemed to be coming from underwater, the words muddled and senseless. Her head weighed about forty pounds, and it was nearly impossible to hold the damn thing up. She slowly blinked her eyes in a futile attempt to force her eyelids to function like windshield wiper blades, hoping to clear her vision enough to discern whether or not the slightly chubby Pete-like figure who had just entered the room was, in fact, her vampire boyfriend, but her forty-pound head suddenly flopped backwards, conking into something hard. Letting her heavy noggin sag at the end of her neck, she awkwardly swung it around to gaze at a knee, which, upon further investigation, she believed to be attached to the older dude sitting behind her.

Angie felt even weirder than she did the time her friend Kell slipped her a tab of acid during the Linkin Park concert when they were nineteen, and she'd felt pretty goddamn weird then. The specific details were lost in the LSD fog, but she had somehow wound up topless onstage with the band, which somehow led to a fistfight with another girl, the resulting brawl spreading throughout a significant portion of the crowd before culminating in Angie's arrest. She sat in a jail cell for three days because her dad — being a wanted criminal and all — wasn't about to risk his own freedom in order to bail her out. Eventually, Kell scrounged the money from a bunch of their friends and sprung Angie from stir. That night during dinner, her dad didn't say a word — no apology, no scolding get-your-shit-together lecture, nothing. She remembered staring at the microwave chicken pot pie he'd lovingly prepared for her, thinking how much better the food had been in jail.

Ugh. She'd have to remember never to tell that story to Pete — at least not the Linkin Park part of it.

Wait — was the older dude sitting behind her actually *her dad?* Angie wrestled her bowling ball of a head back around once again, this time resting her chin on the man's knee — hoping the fragile bones there could handle the awesome weight of her melon — and squinted up at him, considering. The trouble with identifying the guy is that he kept going from male model to Picasso painting and back again. Or was that just the inside of her eyeballs? She hadn't seen her dad in quite some time, but she supposed he could've learned to dress better and gotten a decent haircut for once.

As she stared up at Possible Dad in the chair, Angie struggled to remember how she'd wound up here, on the floor, with a large rock for a head and a brain full of thick liquid. She'd been with Pete, and things were good — or maybe weird, or perhaps even both — and then something happened to the truck... but why were they *in* the truck? And why did she remember *flying?* It was like trying to remember a dream while still dreaming, her furry brain layering images and events on top of one another while melting them all into one. Better to err on the side of caution, before she gets in even deeper trouble.

"Daaad," Angie slurred, smiling up at the man in the chair, "thass Pete, an' thizhizz vampire freyns."

43

In the moments since Fitzgerald pleasantly greeted them, Pete had nearly raised the crossbow and fired, thought better of it for fear of hitting Angie, then changed his mind and was about to take the shot when Angie suddenly called

Fitzgerald *Dad* and introduced Pete and his pals to the vampire.

This whole thing just kept getting weirder.

"We've already met, dear," Fitzgerald said, reaching out to pat Angie on top of the head, his hand trembling a bit in the process.

Not scared. Surely not that. Pete eyed Fitzgerald curiously. The lamp next to the vampire threw more light on his lap than on his face, but even still, Pete could see he looked *wrong*. His skin seemed gray and dry, his cheeks sunken, shadowed half-moons beneath his eyes.

Angie's head flopped back around to smile at Pete. "Heya," she mumbled.

"Hey," Pete said softly, forcing a smile past his worry. "You okay?"

"No, I dunno," Angie said, her head lolling backwards again.

"She's unhurt." Fitzgerald's voice rasped as he spoke. "For the moment."

Something tightened in Pete's chest.

Take the shot.

Pete's finger pressed against the crossbow's trigger, but the weapon remained pointed towards the floor. He'd never fired a gun of any sort in his life, didn't know if he could even hit the wall on the other side of the room, let alone plant the stake in Fitzgerald's chest. *Damn it.* Now that he was standing here fifteen feet away from Fitzgerald, he didn't know what the hell to do. Even sick as Fitzgerald so obviously was, Pete wasn't willing to bet the vampire couldn't move fast enough to tear Angie's throat out before the stake left the crossbow.

Pete caught movement on his left — Pinball inching

forward impatiently, muscles tense, axe poised for the business of hacking. He shot a glance at her, trying to wave her off with a nod of his head. She scowled back at him, bloodlust in her eyes. Could he stop her if she made a run for Fitzgerald? Yeah, that seemed likely. Her biceps were bigger than his neck.

He just wanted to get Angie out of there. Whatever happened after that didn't matter.

No, that wasn't entirely true: Pete wanted to get out of there, too. Self-sacrifice was one thing, and he was fairly bent on it if it wound up being the only way to save Angie, but dammit, he wanted to live through this. He wanted, more than anything else he could possibly imagine, to be with her.

"Please," Pete said, "let Angie go."

His hand still trembling, Fitzgerald stroked Angie's blonde hair. "You can save her, Peter. You know how."

Turn her. Simple enough, right?

If Pete could have looked into his own eyes he would've been shocked at the hatred burning there.

Once upon a time, Pete had dreams, like any other young man. For instance: he'd given some thought to opening a little record store, somewhere down the coast from Los Angeles — San Juan Capistrano, maybe. A nice beach community, quiet, where he could gaze out at the ocean when he wasn't helping customers. And hell, his buddy Hector knew a guy who knew a guy who might've been able to get Pete on as a roadie for America's upcoming tour, circa late 1973, in support of their third album. The band was a little squishy for Pete's taste but it could've led to something. And of course, like any other young man, Pete had dreamed of meeting a groovy chick, settling down.

Fitzgerald killed all that. Pete was good and goddamned

if he'd let him kill anything else he cared about.

Take the shot.

Pinball bumped against Pete's left shoulder, coiled and ready to fight. The shit was very nearly upon the fan, whether he liked it or not. Pete shot a look behind him. Carmella glanced at him, then quickly looked away again, her sword pointed towards the floor, her expression hesitant, no doubt having second thoughts about all this. Elric stood awkwardly leaning to one side, arms dangling, the dagger about to slip from his grasp — the Goth Scarecrow of Oz, worried that a match might soon be struck. He looked to be nearly as dazed as Angie, as if being in Fitzgerald's presence had intoxicated him. Standing near the doorway, Mr. Stovall clutched his vampire-slayer bags and seemed very small and old indeed.

Turning to face Fitzgerald, Pete gave diplomacy one last try. "If you let her go — let all of them go," he said, gesturing towards the other vampires and the old man, "I'll stay here. You can drink my blood till you're about to pop."

His expression souring, Fitzgerald's fingers closed around Angie's hair. She grunted softly but didn't seem to be feeling any pain. The vampire leaned forward in his chair, his face fully in the light for the first time. Pete was stunned. Fitzgerald looked older now than he had when they entered the room, lines gouging his undead gray skin, thin white streaks spiderwebbing his raven hair. *Maybe if I stall long enough*, Pete thought, *the old fucker will just crumble to dust and we can all go home*.

"You feed on *livestock*, Peter," Fitzgerald bitterly croaked. "Your blood would never sustain me." That frigid smile fluttered across the vampire's face again. "But you did a fine job of bringing the others here."

"Say what now?" Pinball snarled. Pete couldn't help but notice her axe blade pivoting towards him. "You set us up?"

"Hell no," Pete insisted. "And if you were paying attention there, you might've caught the part where I offered to sacrifice myself for you guys."

"I can assure you, Peter did nothing untoward," Fitzgerald said, resting a wobbly elbow on the arm of his chair. "But I *am* impressed that he was able to bring some semblance of order from chaos."

Pinball seemed unsure, but at least the axe blade didn't come down on Pete's skull.

Order from Chaos. You know who talked like that? Freaking Blue Oyster Cult and Carson Fitzgerald, that's who.

"The *girl*, Peter," Fitzgerald hissed, his fingers still curled in Angie's hair.

"Yeah, Peter, the girl," Angie repeated, too damned out of it to understand the trouble she was in.

Fitzgerald yanked Angie's head back, exposing her throat. She gasped softly. "Or I can do it, if you like," Fitzgerald said, his cracked lips drawing back to bare his fangs.

Pete's knuckles whitened on the crossbow's handle as rage coursed through him. This was it, time to take his best shot, see if he could put that stake through Fitzgerald's black heart, end this thing once and —

"No!" Mr. Stovall shouted, suddenly shoving past Pete, who responded by pulling the trigger of the crossbow, firing their one-and-only arrow clean through his own right foot and into the floor. The crossbow fell from his hand and he wailed in pain, fairly certain he felt his little toe come loose inside his boot. Pete looked up from the stake protruding from his foot just in time to see Mr. Stovall produce the cross from his smiley-face bag, brandishing it towards Fitzgerald.

A whole lot of things happened very quickly at that point.

A cacophony of snarling and hissing filled the air as every vampire in the room ducked and covered from the cross — except Fitzgerald. Hand in front of his face, peering through his fingers, Pete saw Fitzgerald release his grip on Angie and spring from his seat, landing between the girl and Mr. Stovall. He didn't quite stick the landing, wobbling a bit, but Pete had figured it correctly: the vampire might be sick, but he still had plenty of juice.

"Mr. Stovall, no!" Pete yelled, lunging forward only to come up short as agonizing pain shot upwards from the stake impaling his foot, making his right leg go limp and dropping him painfully to the other knee. Despite being as far away from his heart as it could possibly get, the stake still burned like hell.

Fitzgerald roared furiously as he rushed at Mr. Stovall. Terrified as he was, the old man stood his ground, holding that cross at arm's length towards the advancing vampire.

Between the pain of the stake through his foot and the cross nearby — and yes, his fear for Angie's life — tears welled in Pete's eyes, his vision blurring, but he could still see well enough to realize Fitzgerald was weakening as he neared the old man's cross. Gripping the stake in both hands, Pete strained to tear it loose, but the tip was wedged deep in the wooden floorboards.

Fitzgerald's withered fingers closed around the cross in Mr. Stovall's hand. The vampire's jaw clenched against the pain and a horrible, low groan escaped his throat, his arm shaking violently. Mr. Stovall gasped as blue flames erupted from Fitzgerald's hand, scorching the old man's flesh. Releasing his grip on the cross, Mr. Stovall staggered back as

Fitzgerald hurled the thing away, sending it clattering across the floor at the far end of the room.

Instantly, Pinball bulldozed forward, eager to start swinging her axe. Carmella, a bit more reluctant, also moved forward a few steps, bringing the tip of her sword up, although it seemed more of an attempt to ward off Fitzgerald than to attack him. Elric, unsurprisingly, remained back near the doorway, although he daintily jabbed his dagger in Fitzgerald's direction, doing his part in the battle. Angie, meanwhile, leaned back against Fitzgerald's chair, watching the turmoil unfold, confusion and fear setting in as her wits began to return.

Fitzgerald spun towards Pinball, ducking as her axe blade sheared past his head. His elbow came up, sharply clocking the vampire girl in the side of her head. Pete could see the lights flash off and on in Pinball's eyes as she swayed for an instant, then Fitzgerald's crisped fingers closed around her throat.

Drawing Pinball in close, Fitzgerald hissed into her ear: "I am not *yours* to take." His eyes flicked towards Pete as his head reared back, a snake preparing to strike. Then he buried his fangs in Pinball's neck.

Carmella screamed. Not in anger, but in sheer terror.

A burst of staccato, whimpering gasps bubbled from Pinball's lips as Fitzgerald feasted on her blood. Her muscled arms went limp, the axe falling from her grasp to bang against the floor.

Pete could see the normal, pale-pink hue returning to Fitzgerald's skin as Pinball's blood coursed into his system, the white streaks in his hair fading somewhat, the burnt flesh on his hand beginning to heal.

Forcing himself to his feet, Pete stared at the stake

protruding from his foot. *This is gonna hurt. Real bad.* Taking a firm grip on his right thigh, Pete clenched his teeth together. Howling furiously, he violently jerked his leg upwards, pulling the stake through his foot and freeing himself. The pain was unbearable, sending him reeling backwards to fall against Elric. Both of them tumbled to the floor, Pete still groaning in agony. That little toe was definitely loose in his boot — he felt it rolling around, bumping against the next toe over.

Still feeding, Fitzgerald watched intently as Pete struggled to his feet, glowering at him. Suddenly, the vampire withdrew his fangs from Pinball's throat, smiling at Pete as he let her limp body drop to the floor. She lay there, eyes open and glassy, but still alive — or at least not any more dead than usual. Carmella, the fight entirely gone from her, rushed to crouch at Pinball's side.

Pete limped a few steps towards Fitzgerald, the two vampires staring each other down like gunfighters. Some of the color had returned to Fitzgerald's flesh, but there was no doubt the sickness still had him in its grasp — the skin of his burned hand remained only partially healed, the steady progress of the pink, new skin stalled, leaving the hand looking waxy and rotten.

Mr. Stovall stood watching nearby, his own burned hand cradled in the other, the smiley-face bag dangling from around his neck.

"Now then," Fitzgerald said. With that, he turned, bent, and — with surprising care — lifted Angie in his arms.

"Pete?" she said, disoriented, still under Fitzgerald's sway.

"Please," Pete begged, staggering forward another couple steps, "put her down. Leave her alone."

An oddly strangulated look spread over Fitzgerald's face, accompanied by soft animal-like grunts. Coarse black fur sprouted from his face and hands, fingernails becoming claws.

Transforming. The son of a bitch is gonna bolt, and take Angie with him. Pete limped forward. "Angie!"

Bones crackling, Fitzgerald rapidly gained a good six inches in height, his clothes shredding away as his body transformed — a sure sign of how sick he was, Pete knew; he sure as hell didn't understand how it worked, but something about the vampirism carried the clothes as well as the body through the transformation — it was why Dracula didn't have to walk around naked after flapping his way into the bedroom of an unsuspecting lass, but it wasn't happening for Fitzgerald.

Slinging Angie over one shoulder, Fitzgerald roared like an enraged grizzly as he spread his arms to display the thin, leathery wings stretching from waist to wrist. His shoes ruptured, exposing massive clawed feet. Wind tore through the room as the half-bat, half-man monstrosity flapped once, twice, going airborne but struggling to gain altitude. Bits and pieces of clothing remained here and there, tattered and stretched across Fitzgerald's retooled body.

Pete grabbed the smiley-face bag from Mr. Stovall's neck, took a bad step on his injured foot, almost fell, then hurled himself forward. His fingers caught fur on the monster's back and he clung there, staring up into Angie's plaintive eyes. Fitzgerald faltered, the added weight nearly pulling him out of the air, but a powerful sweep of his wings got him moving again. The clump of fur in Pete's hand tore loose. Plummeting, Pete desperately clutched for anything, narrowly catching hold of Fitzgerald's belt as the gigantic bat-creature neared the skylight, huge wings beating force-fully. His face way too close to Fitzgerald's ass for anyone's comfort, Pete was grateful the shredded scraps of the bat-creature's pants remained in place.

The beast hit the skylight. Pete ducked his head as the ceiling shattered, chunks of the skylight and its framework tumbling past him. A fragment of glass razored the denim on Pete's left leg, cutting into the flesh. The house grew smaller as they gained altitude, the tiny figure of Mr. Stovall visible through the wrecked skylight, peering upwards.

Shaking glass from his hair, Pete looked up, worried that Angie had been sliced to ribbons. A few small cuts marred the exposed skin of her arms, but she seemed okay other-wise. Fitzgerald's hypnotic effect was fading, however, her bewilderment fast becoming stark terror.

Okay — now what? Pete thought for sure his jumping aboard would've been too much for Fitzgerald to handle in his obviously weakened state, but the big bat was still gain-ing altitude and heading towards the heart of Hollywood. As he desperately fought to come up with some kind of plan — the huge failing of this entire endeavor having been the complete lack of any sort of strategy, he realized — Pete's eyes darted from Angie's frightened expression to the land-scape below and up to the unfocused sphere of the moon, glimmering through the haze overhead. *So I was riding along on the ass of a giant vampire bat, the woman I love dangling from the monster's shoulder, and I've got no clue where we're going or how to correct the situation.* Perfect.

Then something twinkled in the Hollywood sky.

Pete's gaze zeroed on the flashing red light. The Capitol Records building on Vine, just north of Hollywood Boule-vard — and directly in their current flight path.

The instantly-recognizable thirteen-story tower — looking not unlike a stack of records on a turntable — featured the biggest damn pointy thing in the city rising from its roof: a 150-foot antenna spire, the red beacon perched at its tip constantly flashing the word *Hollywood* in morse code.

Pete looked up at Angie again, staring into her terrified eyes… and an inexplicable wave of calm washed over him. "I'm gonna get you out of this," he shouted against the wind and the thunderous beating of Fitzgerald's wings.

"Okay," she said, eyes wide, working hard to wrestle her fear into submission. "How 'bout now?"

Pete smiled at her, even as his wave of calm hit the rocks to splatter away into quivering puddles of *Oh-Fuck-Now-I've-Gotta-Make-This-Work*. His plan — the word itself probably giving it too much credit — was going to require an astonishing fusion of coordination and pure luck, neither of those being things Pete was known for. Not to mention he figured the chances were extremely high that Angie would never want to speak to him again even if he managed to pull it off.

Still gripping Fitzgerald's belt with his right hand, Pete slipped the strap of the smiley-face bag over his neck. It occurred to Pete that Fitzgerald had made very little attempt to shake him off, and in fact, seemed perfectly content with his passenger. It was unsettling, to say the least. He nervously eyed Fitzgerald's monstrous head, praying the vampire wouldn't get curious and glance over his shoulder to see what Pete was up to back there in the vicinity of his hairy butt.

For her part, Angie was *mighty* curious as to what Pete was up to, watching intently as Pete used his free hand to dig into the bag, carefully withdrawing a wooden stake. Lifting the stake to his mouth, he clenched it between his teeth and reached into the bag again, this time coming up with the hammer — which he promptly fumbled. The hammer, plummeting exactly like a dropped hammer, banged painfully into Pete's kneecap, bounced off the pierced toe of his right boot, then quickly disappeared from sight as it plunged into the streets of Hollywood. Pete stared after it, heart sinking. *Please don't let that hit anybody*.

Well, he hadn't been quite sure how he was going to pound a stake into Fitzgerald's back with one hand, anyway.

Besides, all he needed was a good distraction.

They were coming up quick on the Capitol Records building, on a course to pass above and slightly to the west of it. This would take some maneuvering.

The stake still firmly gripped in his teeth, Pete looked into Angie's face once more. Not surprisingly, she appeared to be scared as hell, but holding it together. Counting on Pete. Had anyone ever done that before? Could he live up to it?

Wordlessly, Pete reached his free hand towards her. Understanding, she took the hand, squeezing it tight. "Nee boaf," he mumbled around the stake in his mouth. "Boaf hanss."

A bit confused, Angie released her grip on Fitzgerald's furry side and grabbed Pete's wrist, balancing precariously over Fitzgerald's shoulder.

Pete cocked his head at her — *Ready?* Angie nodded back, her grip tightening on Pete's hand and wrist.

Don't screw this up, he told himself. Then he let go of Fitzgerald's belt, felt himself slipping as Angie struggled to maintain her hold on him. With his free hand, he snatched the stake from his teeth. Glanced up to see Fitzgerald look back over his shoulder.

Pete drew back, then plunged the stake into Fitzgerald's side. The wood sank deep into the soft meat just below the rib cage.

Fitzgerald shrieked, body twisting in the air. Angie slipped off the bat-thing's shoulder, both she and Pete in free-fall now —

And Pete began to transform.

It was about as close to pure agony as Pete could imagine. Bones reshaped themselves, muscle stretching, writhing, twisting. His clothes shredded away from his body — apparently that business of the clothes transforming along with the flesh had something to do with *practice* as well as the health of the vampire — to reveal his fuzzy, chubby bat-belly, and very nearly expose portions of himself he'd prefer to keep under wraps, furry or not. As his boots tore away from his clawed, bat-like feet, Pete saw his severed little toe — still human — tumbling towards the street below. He felt his facial features distort, becoming monstrous, then saw the leaf-shaped bat nose form at the end of his snout.

Mortified, Pete looked at Angie, but her gaze was focused on the skin beneath his arms as it expanded and stretched, becoming wings. Frantically, he drew Angie in, transferring her to his shoulder, where she found handholds in the rather embarrassing forest of back fur he'd sprouted. He shot an anxious look at her. She stared into his eyes, buried within his gruesome face. *I'm still in here*, he wanted to shout.

Hoping Angie had a good grip on him, Pete thrust his arms — wings, *wings* — out to either side, the sudden lift as he caught air battering him violently and sending him rocketing upwards, as if he'd pulled the cord on a parachute. He and Angie both hollered wildly, the muscles in Pete's arms and back tensing as he struggled to gain some kind of control. This flying shit was tougher than you'd think.

Below, Fitzgerald was swirling out of the sky like a bomber with a wing blown off. Screaming with rage, the vampire clawed at the stake jutting from his side, red eyes drilling through Pete. Beyond, that beacon atop the Capitol Records building continued flashing: *Hollywood... Hollywood...*

If Pete didn't catch Fitzgerald — and fast — this whole thing was going to fall apart. *"Hold on tight!"* he yelled at Angie, instantly regretting it when he heard his thick, snarling voice. Feeling her fingers dig deeper into his back-fur, Pete hoped like hell what he was about to do wouldn't send them crash-diving into the roof of a building, then threw his arms up and back. This had the effect of opening an invisible trap door beneath his feet, sending Pete and Angie dropping rapidly towards Fitzgerald — perhaps a bit more rapidly than Pete had intended, but with slight movements of his arms (*wings*, dammit), he was able to ease the fall into something more like a controlled dive. *Barely* controlled, yes, but it was all about the baby steps.

With Angie's weight throwing off his balance and his little gut protruding into his view, Pete didn't feel particularly aerodynamic, but damned if he wasn't able to aim himself. They were moving in fast on Fitzgerald, who was still spiraling downwards. Targeting a spot he hoped would wind up being dead-center in Fitzgerald's back, Pete dipped his wings back again, increasing his speed. Then — an instant before impact — Pete spread his wings wide, slowing down but still hitting Fitzgerald with one hell of a body-slam. Fitzgerald snarled angrily, spittle flying from his lips, his clawed hands swiping at Pete. Feeling damnably freakish, Pete gripped Fitzgerald in his bat-feet — left foot on the vampire's side, near the stake, right foot at his shoulder, like a surfer riding a wave — leaving his hands (and wings) free so he could pilot Fitzgerald to his final destination.

Fitzgerald kicked and twisted, trying to squirm free of Pete's grip, making it even tougher for Pete to control his flight and very nearly causing him to go into another dive. Pete felt like his arms were about to tear from their sockets as he fought to stay on course, heading straight for that red beacon.

Hollywood… Hollywood…

The spire atop the Capitol Records building loomed below. Pete suddenly felt like a suicidal fish hurling itself towards the fisherman's spear, not sure he'd be able to time this right and avoid impaling all three of them.

Finally realizing what was coming, Fitzgerald's struggling grew more frantic, but it was too late. Fitzgerald roared as Pete released his grip on the vampire, simultaneously extending his wings to hit the brakes. The spire punched into Fitzgerald's gut and through his back, destroying a large section of his torso as the vampire's momentum drove him several feet downwards on the metal antenna. Pete dipped his left wing in a desperate attempt to dodge away, the tip of the spire hammering his arm and knocking him off-balance. Jarred by the impact, Angie lost her grip on Pete's fur, screaming as she tumbled away towards the building's roof.

Wings back, wincing at the pain, Pete dove for Angie. Catching her wrist in his right hand, he quickly enfolded her in his wing, drawing her in towards his chest. Holding her tightly — oh-so-tightly — that way, he used his other wing to slowly corkscrew them down to the roof, like a kid's parachute toy spinning out of the sky on tangled strings. They didn't hit the roof gently, but Pete was able to take the brunt of the impact, rolling awkwardly before coming to a stop on his back, wings spread out, Angie sprawled across his chest. Hurriedly, Pete slithered from beneath her, getting to his feet and staggering away, groaning as he painfully returned to human form.

Ashamed, he glanced back at her over his no-longer-quite-as-furry shoulder. "Are you okay?"

"I... I think," Angie said, sitting up. "Are you?"

As Pete started to worry about just what that question might mean, a horrifying shriek split the air, drawing their attention upwards.

Fitzgerald, blood coursing from his torn midsection and flowing down the spire, clutched at the slick metal with his clawed hands. Slowly, agonizingly — hands slipping and sliding — he began pushing himself upwards.

Pete and Angie stared, stunned, as Fitzgerald inched his body up the metal shaft, glowering down at them the entire time.

"God *damn* it," Angie hollered, getting to her feet. "How can that guy not be *dead?*"

"Metal," Pete said. "It's metal. You can't just stick any ol' thing through a vampire and have it kill him, but it was so big I thought it might do the trick anyway." He kicked at a junction box on the roof, wincing as his bare foot connected with it. "SHIT," he swore miserably.

Up above, Fitzgerald's hands slipped in his blood and he slid several inches down the spire, howling in pain, before catching hold of it again. Wheezing, he pushed himself further up, nearer and nearer to the spire's tip.

"You got more stakes in there?" Angie nodded towards the smiley-face bag, still slung around Pete's neck. "Just fly up and stake the shit out of him once and for all."

Pete stared at her, confused. "But you —" He held up his hands, looked at them, then back at Angie. "It's so… disgusting and freaky," he muttered.

The compassion in Angie's face surprised him. "Pete," she said, walking towards him, her eyes focused on his. "You're the most human guy I've ever met. But you can also do some crazy shit, and now —" she looked up at Fitzgerald, getting closer and closer to freeing himself from the spire — "now would be a very good time to do a little more."

Pete searched her face, desperate to be certain. "All right," he said. "But just do me one favor — *don't watch*."

Angie turned away, staring out at the lights of Hollywood, a huge vampire bat squirming atop the Capitol Records building above her, her boyfriend turning into a similar creature behind her.

And she didn't watch, even as Pete yelped and hollered during the transformation.

But she did whisper "Be careful."

Pete remembered to dig a stake from Mr. Stovall's smiley-face bag *before* taking flight. Then, stake held tightly in his clawed right hand, he gave a tremendous flap of his wings, kicking up dust from the rooftop as he went airborne. He glanced down at Angie, standing with her back turned, and wished she weren't perched so close to the edge of the rooftop. Safety first, and all that.

Despite his continued uncertainty as to how the flying thing worked, Pete nonetheless quickly closed the distance between the rooftop and Fitzgerald at the tip of the spire. As Pete approached, he saw Fitzgerald's gaze flick to the stake in his hand, the vampire's demeanor softening, becoming almost serene.

Pete flew up and past Fitzgerald, thought about trying to perch on the tip of the spire, decided he was too clumsy for that, then awkwardly landed on the vampire's back. His weight forced Fitzgerald further down on the blood-drenched spire, the metal goring him deeper. A soft moan escaped his lips.

"I'm sorry," Pete whispered, feeling like he was going to throw up. He crouched, fought for balance, and raised the stake above his head, clenching it in both hands.

Fitzgerald hung his head limply, his eyes closing. "That's the boy," he rasped. "That's the boy..."

Pete put everything he had into the thrust. The stake entered Fitzgerald's back, glancing off the left shoulder blade and plunging deep past the spine, smashing ribs out of its way before sinking into Fitzgerald's heart.

Pete fell as the body exploded into ash. He flailed for a moment before his wings caught air, then glided gently down to the rooftop amidst the falling ash, pleased to see that Angie still had her back turned.

As his feet met the rooftop, Pete wasted no time returning to human form. When his grunts and yelps abated, he said "You can look now."

Angie turned, gazing up at the spire through what looked like falling snow. Then she looked at Pete, a bit stupefied. "I guess that's one dead vampire."

Pete stepped towards her. "I'm sorry you..." he began, clutching what was left of his tattered jeans to himself, "...I'm sorry for *everything*."

She quickly walked to him, sinking her fingers into his little 'fro, and kissed him.

Right on his used-to-be-bat lips.

44

Once they'd heard the news about Fitzgerald, Carmella had extended a free-drinks-for-life offer to Mr. Stovall and his wife. For the sake of politeness, they'd taken her up on it the very next night, but Club Emoglobin was too loud and crazy for the old couple — and besides, it seemed like the kind of place a fellow like William Petersen might hang out, and Mr. Stovall didn't want the trouble. They'd each quickly consumed one drink — again, to be polite — then said their goodbyes to Carmella, Elric and Pinball before retreating once again to their cozy apartment. Mr. Stovall didn't need a reward, anyway — he was just glad to have been of use. And Pete had even returned his smiley-face bag.

* * *

Pinball watched the old man and his wife amble down the sidewalk into the Sunset Boulevard night. She still wasn't feeling a hundred percent after Fitzgerald feasted on her, and she hoped like hell he hadn't given her whatever his sickness was through the bite, but overall, she felt pretty solid. Good enough to kick the shit out of anyone who might get out of line at the bar, that's for sure. Leaving the crowd of Emoglobin hopefuls lined up outside, she pulled the door open and entered the club.

Pinball shouldered through the crowd, watching Elric as the narrow vampire tended bar. He must have been in a celebratory mood, because he was sporting the most god-awful shirt she'd ever seen him in, a velour monstrosity with puffy sleeves and some kind of colorful nonsense — she wasn't sure if it was flowers or birds or images of Satan — embroidered all over it. A perky Goth girl — such a thing existed — accepted the drink Elric had poured, sipping it and grinning at the vampire. He'd been utterly useless in the fight, but he did mix a mean cocktail.

Entering the back corridor, Pinball walked to the ornate door at the end and knocked.

"S'open," Carmella said.

Pinball opened the door, but didn't enter. Inside the room, Carmella was seated on the velvet couch, alone, a drink in her hand.

"We're at capacity," Pinball reported.

"Okay," Carmella said flatly. She stared at Pinball for a long moment. "Shouldn't we feel different?"

"Probably," Pinball said. "Lemme know if you need anything." She pulled the door closed and headed back down the corridor, towards the thumping beat and the would-be vampires dancing their little hearts out.

45

Pete's Duster was parked in a pull-out overlooking the ocean off the Pacific Coast Highway near Malibu, Cheap Trick's cover of *California Man* wailing from the radio. Nearby, Pete and Angie sat on a blanket spread on the ground, gazing out at the moonlight reflecting on the waves, a wadded up Fatburger sack between them.

Pete had wisely chosen not to eat a Fatburger but enjoyed watching Angie devour hers. He still felt more than a little squirmy after the events of the previous night, especially having turned into a creepy giant bat in front of her. "You sure you don't mind hanging out with a guy who can, you know — do what I did last night?" he asked, nervous.

Angie swigged from a bottle of beer and smiled at him. "Just keep bein' sweet to me and I don't care what kinda rodent you wanna turn into." She cocked an eyebrow at him. "Bat's a rodent, right?"

"I guess," Pete said.

Why couldn't he shake this feeling of unease? Everything had gone surprisingly well — which, of course, was exactly why Pete was gnawing at himself. Fitzgerald had barely put up a fight, and Pete didn't believe it was simply because the vampire was sick. *That's the boy*, Fitzgerald had said. Had he somehow set Pete up, manipulating him all the way to the end? And if so, *why?* It was damned disturbing.

"You in there?"

Shaking it off, Pete found himself gazing at Angie's smiling face. Who needs sunlight when they've got that? "Just thinkin' about stuff, sorry."

"No problem," Angie said. "I mean, it's not like you went through a major life-changing event less than twenty-four hours ago or something."

Pete frowned. "I just can't shake it, the way Fitzgerald — it was like he didn't want to bother anymore, y'know? I swear he almost looked peaceful when I was about to put that stake in him."

"Suicide by vampire?" Angie suggested.

"There's somethin' more to it, but I sure don't know what. I think I did exactly what he wanted — he forced me to go full-vampire-bozo to save you, whether it was by turning you or doing the…" Pete looked away, embarrassed. "…The bat thing."

Grinning, Angie bumped her shoulder against his. "You said *save me*."

"I said save *you*," Pete corrected.

"My chubby vampire hero." She slipped an arm around him.

Pete leaned his head against hers, feeling his apprehension quietly tiptoeing away. Everything was fine. Probably. Pete relaxed, enjoying the warmth coming off Angie's body, the smell of her making him tingle. "My toe's growing back already — wanna see?"

"Yuck," Angie said.

They stared out at the sea for a moment, then Angie lifted her head to look at Pete, mischief in her eyes. "You wanna go steal a goat?"

SCOTT S. PHILLIPS has written all kinds of stuff: films, TV, books, comics and even dialogue for talking dolls. He's the author of the *Pete, Drinker of Blood* series, as well as *Man with Chihuahua* and several other books. Under the pen name Stevie Jordan Pawminter, Scott cowrites (with Sarah Bartsch) the Danger Potato cozy mystery series (book one, *Wicked Snarl*, is out now, book two coming soon) and the Sniff and Nibble cozy mystery series (book one coming soon).

Perhaps most importantly, he once performed as stand-in for the legendary Lemmy in the video for Motorhead's "Sacrifice."

Please visit Scott's Patreon page (patreon.com/scott_s_phillips), where you can get cool exclusives like sneak peeks at chapters of upcoming books, a Patrons-only blog, read Scott's monthly terrible poems (and see videos of him doing dramatic readings of those very same terrible poems), get your name listed in the acknowledgements of his books, and even have a character named after you!

You can also find Scott at Facebook (facebook.com/scottphillipsnm).

Made in United States
Troutdale, OR
01/05/2024

16704709R00148